M.C.

Iris Nolan (nee Dickens) spent her early childhood on a Wairarapa sheep station. She graduated M.A. (Hons) from Victoria University. Her first book was published in 1938. Later she taught post-primary students for sixteen years wherever her husband's local body appointments took the family of son and daughter. *Bells for Caroline* won the BNZ/Women Writers' Award for first historical novel.

A GOOD MAN'S LOVE

Elizabeth Harris

Hal Dillon and Ben MacAllister had been deeply affected by the appalling death of their university friend Laurie. Hal journeyed to Mexico to continue his anthropological studies, and there found distraction in his passionate affair with Magdalena. But was he inviting even more heartache? Ben became a wanderer. While working in Cyprus he had met English girl Jo Daniel, and, after a nomadic summer together, they travelled to England to embark on what promised to be a lifetime of marital bliss. But Jo discovers that promises don't always come true.

HOT POPPIES

Reggie Nadelson

A murder in New York's diamond district. A dead Chinese girl with a photograph in her pocket. A plastic bag of irradiated heroin in an empty apartment. A fire in a Chinatown sweatshop. The worst blizzard in New York's history. These events conspire to bring ex-cop Artie Cohen out of retirement and back into the obsessive world of murder and politics that nearly killed him. The terrifying plot uncoils first in New York — in Artie's own back yard — then in Hong Kong, where everything — and everyone — is for sale.

Other titles in the
Ulverscroft Large Print Series:

STRANGER IN THE PLACE

Anne Doughty

Elizabeth Stewart, a Belfast student and only daughter of hardline Protestant parents, sets out on a study visit to the remote west coast of Ireland. Delighted as she is by the beauty of her new surroundings and the small community which welcomes her, she soon discovers she has more to learn than the details of the old country way of life. She comes to reappraise so much that is slighted and dismissed by her family — not least in regard to herself. But it is her relationship with a much older, Catholic man, Patrick Delargy, which compels her to decide what kind of life she really wants.

IF HE LIVED

Jon Stephen Fink

Lillian is a woman who feels too much. As a psychiatric nurse, she empathizes with her patients; as a mother, she mourns for her lost, runaway daughter. Now suddenly she has a new feeling, that her house, one of the oldest in the small Massachusetts town where she lives with her husband Freddy, has been invaded, violated by some past evil. And then Lillian sees the boy . . .

1

Dark shawls over their heads, the women waited at the pithead in dreary resignation. The crying, the keening, the disbelief was over. Gaunt bleary-eyed miners shook their heads. The shaft, where those not underground during the cave-in had worked so frantically for the previous two days, was silent.

The murmurs, the outcries, the threats against the manager were forgotten, as he explained grimly that there was no hope of rescuing those trapped; no signals showed that any were still alive. He would risk no more men; the rescuers had heard the surge of breakers where no roar of sea had echoed before.

An old man who had seen similar collapses in other areas said abruptly, 'So they've been buried. When d'ye re-open the mine, Josh Tremaine? There's two days pay lost, and the children without food.'

'Shut your mouth, Cal. A lot you care for our sons and daughters,' snarled a toothless crone. 'It's your booze ye'd be wanting.'

Josh's quiet voice silenced them. 'This

1

mine will not re-open. I'll not re-open, it, I swear. There's no money for shoring timber. I'll send no man down there again without it.'

'We could sink another shaft,' Cal said.

'You'll have to find work somewhere else,' Josh disregarded the interruption. 'I've paid you all I could. It's finished.'

'All the mines near here are closed,' said another.

'You greedy beggars' shouted an almost hysterical young woman. 'You've got your two hands. And where's my man?'

'And mine?'

'And mine?'

'And mine?'

Eight echoes, as the newly widowed, shaken from their anguish by Cal's unfeeling cruelty, exploded in fury against the manager. Forgotten now the fact that he had kept their mine open, when, with the price of tin collapsing, others closed one after the other. The owner was a being far out of their reach in his carriage and his castle; but this man Josh Tremaine had been a foreman before the mine fell into the hands of an idle eldest son who cared nothing for the safety of his workmen. They knew Josh, he had grown up and gone down to the vein of ore beside them. There he was. Unfair though it was, the blame for the dangerous adits and shafts could be laid on his shoulders.

Standing apart, his gentle wife with her black shawl over her head moved as if to speak.

Josh turned to her. 'Go home to our daughter, Jennie, she needs you. You can do no good here now. Perhaps in a week or two they may let you help.'

She drifted quietly off, away from the close-knit village. According to her now deceased parents, she had 'married beneath her'. That the young man with whom she had fallen in love was thoughtful, clean-living, well-mannered, on his way to being a mine manager sometime did not count. Strangely for a shy girl of that day and age, she was determined to marry him, however much the family might try to dissuade her. In the end threats of eloping forced them to agree although reluctantly to the wedding.

Mrs Tremaine was not thinking of her earlier days now. What would she tell Mary, the chubby girl in pretty clothes, brought up in the second decade of Queen Victoria's reign, unaware like most remote villagers of the war in the Crimea? With her dark curls and dancing feet, joyous for no reason and every reason, she was the darling of her parents' hearts. Bitter cold of winter meant only the possible delights of a heavy snowfall.

The comfortable home was always warm with glowing coals, the thick stone walls keeping out the fierce gales that raged over the Peninsula. They had guarded her from the seamier side of life, but insisted on a sound education at the local school. The private boarding school which her mother had attended was beyond both their means and their status.

Just as they protected Mary from nature's savagery, so they wanted to protect her from the cruelty of the mining tragedy. School was closed for a month, her mother thought thankfully. Her little daughter would hear soon enough about the disaster, and probably she would be told that her father caused it. Children often abetted by adults could be vicious; life so far had been very kind to Mary in that pleasant cottage.

Josh had been anxious this last year, trying to keep his men safe and in work, but he did not voice his concern at home. Yet he could not screw a penny out of the skinflint mine owner for timber.

'Shoring pays no dividends,' the latter had said pompously. 'You are paid to keep the mine going. There's little enough profit in it now. You'll have to think about cutting wages. Or give some of them the sack. They don't work hard enough.'

'They've all been in your mine longer than me,' Josh said. 'Father and son, and grandfather before them.'

'If you won't keep it going, I'll find someone who will!' the owner had threatened.

Put that way Josh had no choice. He could find work himself despite the fact that many mines were closed. But a stranger would not consider the miners.

The owner had not dared to cut Josh's pay. Even his wife had only a vague suspicion that a large proportion of her husband's wages contributed to others less able to cope: days off with the miners' bugbear, bronchitis, a brood of youngsters, an ailing wife or a dying elderly parent.

The manager had grown more worried this last year as the miners burrowed ever deeper, following a payable vein of ore. He had often gone down himself, listening to that increasing roar of the sea, too close in those honeycombed cliffs. A day or two before the collapse he had suggested the miners stop until somehow he found shoring timber. They were too deep, too near the coast; he thought they might be under the sea itself.

Cal, the man with no sympathy for the recently widowed, had sneered. 'Man and boy, I've worked this mine for fifty years. You might be the godalmighty manager, but you don't know this mine like I do, you've only been here ten years or so. All the shafts are safe.'

This acknowledged local leader could not be disregarded. 'Look,' Josh said, 'I've worked in mines with rock walls. Here there's weak strata where shoring-up's needed, and the owner won't supply the timber, even from his own plantings.'

'We need our pay,' Cal said. 'We'll work here even if you're too lily-livered.' He knew that Josh was in charge at the pit-head, but he rejoiced at the opportunity of insulting him.

Returning to the surface, Josh decided to try once more to persuade the owner to cut trees from his own parkland to shore that particular shaft. He was sure it ran out to the weather-beaten and eroded cliffs. Some trees could be spared, surely, some past their best or not suitable for anything but rough timber.

If that effort failed, he would try to persuade the men to sink another shaft further inland. Perhaps they could follow the vein in that safer direction.

Neither argument succeeded. The men knew the mine would stay open only if they could bring up a good quantity of ore quickly.

So eight men died needlessly. And the rest were without work.

Grumblings from the survivors grew louder. Why did he close the mine? They could have followed another lode. Why didn't he supply the timber to make the adits safer? Bolder, they stared at the woman until she felt threatened even in the tiny church.

Her husband became more morose; home, that used to be so bright, dull and cold.

Soon Mary was told that her schooldays were over. She did not mind; the few children now attending pinched her when Teacher was not looking, tore her books, took her lunch. She began to suspect the teacher did not want to notice. When the mine had been working, no-one was so praised as the manager's daughter; now, no-one could be so quickly scolded for careless work, torn books, grubby dresses where stones had been flung, forgetfulness. If Mary dared argue, she was clipped over the ears as the others had been. It was another world.

Presently her father found work in a more distant mine, staying away from home all week. Mother was quiet and withdrawn. Pieces of furniture disappeared. No new frocks came Mary's way.

Far from being sympathetic, the widows grew arrogant. If a son threw a stone with accuracy, the window remained shattered. The village policeman could or would never

7

find the culprit. Seedlings in the poor soil mother now tilled vanished over night, at the right moment for replanting. As a result the widows' gardens in the village produced more vegetables than they ever had when the menfolk were alive.

Mother grew thin and pale, slow-moving where before she had been quicksilver. Mary, no longer singing merrily round the house with her dark curls gleaming, watched helplessly as the weeks went by, her father returning less frequently. The comfortable stone cottage, pleasantly large but no castle, was colder. Less food appeared on the table.

Perhaps Mary would appreciate the company of other people, mother suggested, where she could earn a little money. She could sew neatly; the local landowner, owner of the collapsed mine, had made it known that his wife had a vacancy for a seamstress. In her neatest clothes Mary presented herself, but was turned away from the front door by a pompous butler who, in the past, had removed her mother's wraps and taken her father's hat as if he were proud to be allowed to do so.

Yes, for a shilling a week she could do all the mending and making. She would be fed and have a bed in the attic where the storms whistled. She must do exactly as she was told,

8

first by the mistress of the castle, then by the housekeeper, and finally by the haughty daughters, older than Mary but gracious friends two years earlier.

The widows never grumbled about this mine owner. He was out of reach. Not so the lonely manager's wife, soon the manager's widow, when he had unwisely, or deliberately? attempted to walk along the coastline in a raging storm during a spring tide. The world Mary had known, already crumbling, vanished with her father.

She was rarely allowed to go home; her working day ran from daylight till dark seven days a week.

After six months, with a golden sovereign in her hand (the rest had been withheld for using a candle, or too much thread, or cutting material too generously) she walked home. So overgrown was the neat garden she did not recognise it; broken windows, cobwebs over the once shining panes, the thatch so threadbare it seemed wetter inside than out. In the dingy bare room mother, almost a stranger, coughed weakly.

She tried to rouse herself when, Mary fearful, bent over her.

'Child, I'm glad to see you. Make a fire. Break the legs off that chair, it'll not be wanted for visitors.'

'There's no need, mother. I have money, the shop will have some coal,' and she ran back towards the village.

She did not hear her mother call, 'He'll not sell you anything, even for a gold sovereign you might have.'

The shopkeeper, who had known Mary since she was a tiny tot, shook his head. He had no coal, no kindling, he told her, though she could see firing in his yard. Had she stolen the sovereign? he asked. He would call the 'Peeler' if she did not leave at once.

A turnip would make soup, she thought; turnips in the field beside her. Horrifying stories she had heard in the 'Big House' made her pause. If you could be transported on a convict ship to Van Diemen's Land for stealing a loaf of bread, what would happen if someone saw you with a turnip? You could explain that your mother was sick, and you had a sovereign you had earned. But would they believe you? Would anyone believe you? Mary did not know that the last convict ship had sailed over ten years earlier — and if she had known she would not have been sure such a punishment as transportation would not start again at the whim of some over-bearing landlord. She could not help her mother much; it would be worse if she was sent across those savage seas. She had lived and cleaned, and still the cottage was not as bright as it had been.

She knew that Bill and Joe were more important to Molesworth than she was. If only she and Irwin had a whare to themselves — Ken was all right, he was clean and tidy. But the other two — they brought to the meal table the dust of hot days, the smell of wild cattle and the sweat of horses. If they shot rabbits for the pot, the blood would have dripped all over their clothes.

Mary was festering with hatred of the place, her job, the men; and Irwin, though he did not speak of it, did, for once, understand. Her obvious feelings made Ken's decision easier to accept.

He told her he would leave the run after they had driven the last of the sale cattle down to Hanmer. Elliot had sold his holding to two sheep farmers of the Waiau Valley, as they had heard when they reached Blenheim. Ken was still sure the country was unsuitable for sheep; what had been whispered of one of the brothers convinced him that, if true, he could not work for the Peninsula dealer. Bill and Joe could stay on, this coming winter; and Irwin and his wife if they wished. The Trelissicks said nothing to Ken, or to each other. The subject was not discussed.

Going to call Irwin in for a meal — usually

she banged an old rusty bucket that the house cow had kicked out of shape — Mary noticed the shape of rockers he was fashioning, too short and too deep for a rocking-chair which he had promised her 'some day'.

'What are those for?' she asked. 'Not a cradle, anyway.' Although she could joke, she still felt that her childless state was a slur. Large families were expected of pioneer women, as she realised.

'Yes,' said Irwin, unthinking, 'it's a cradle.'

Mary's face lost its colour. 'The only thing I can't do as a pioneer, and you have to hold it against me! There are times when I think I hate you,' she added furiously, turning away to hide tears more of rage than disappointment.

'What have I done?' he asked impatiently. Having found two pieces of timber beside the whare, he had been working happily for hours. Did Mary suspect he was going prospecting? 'No, don't you walk away, woman, what's the matter with making a cradle?'

'Who's it for?' she snapped. 'Some woman you met when you and Ken rode to Blenheim?'

'Don't be stupid, girl.' His face cleared. 'Why would I make a cradle for anyone there? Jean has her own, and Ray and Polly will be well set up. This is a miner's cradle.'

'Miner's cradle — for you? Or for Ken?'

'Ken, anyway,' he replied, not yet admitting that he also planned to look for gold.

He turned back to the bench, and Mary had to be content with his answer. Where would he find another part plank for the box? He would need matting, perhaps they could leave that for Blenheim, and the riffles, too. But he really wanted to complete the one piece of equipment he could make. It was Ken who reminded him that the packhorses would have full loads without the completed cradle.

'We'll pack the parts out,' Ken said. 'Then we'll decide how to carry it to the Wakamarina. Did Tom tell you some of the men are sailing from Nelson to Linkwater, then foot-slogging up the valley from Havelock?'

'But you wouldn't sail from Blenheim, Ken?'

'No, of course not. We'll cross over the Wairau at Renwick Town, go up the Kaituna Valley. It should be a good track, a few hundred were taking off when we left. I just hope we won't be too late.'

8

They waited impatiently for the earliest date on which they could set off to round up the cattle. As Ken had said in the spring, Irwin needed all that experience of droving over Barefells Pass. This time, though he led the packhorses to the huts near the high tops, he was in the saddle on all the round-ups. The more difficult gullies fell to the lot of Bill and Joe, with Ken handling hidden pockets where the beasts seemed to know the dogs would want to avoid the matagouri. Irwin would be there with a stockwhip and two of Ken's dogs, to stop the bellowing groups from milling back. It was hot, the expected 80 degrees, the sun reflected from bare rocks near the tops, and muggy in the valleys.

The men slept uncomfortably in that short interval between pitch dark and daybreak on tussock layers spread on the earth floor. Even in sleep Irwin heard stockwhips crack, dogs bark and cattle bellow. But they brought them down to the winter pastures with not many left behind. The owner wanted most of them sold. Henry Caton would be bringing his own stock onto Molesworth, Ken had been informed.

Near the dwelling the noisome smell of singed hide told its own tale of branding, a most awkward business without really efficient yards. Bill and Joe were delighted, roping the steers in the race and throwing them. Irwin was busy with the fire, keeping the branding-iron hot; Ken would lean over the fence, the long iron handle allowing him to burn the Elliott insignia into the beast's hide without climbing into the race. Joe had learnt from an earlier near disaster to perch on the railings, rickety though they were. If an enraged five hundredweight of bullock leaned against him, he would be jammed in an unpleasant and probably fatal position. The few late calves still at foot were easy to handle, but once weaned their harsh blaring echoed round the hills for days. All work would stop while Irwin belted yet another slab of wood into place, where the shoulders of a frightened beast had lunged against the fence.

Three days saw the task finished. The young heifers, capable of producing better calves when mated with Langridge bulls, would be driven down the Awatere when the drovers returned from their trip to Hanmer with that station's outgoing beasts. This winter there would be few cattle on the lower pastures, leaving fresh growth for Caton's stock. Ken still did not know whether the new lessee would be bringing sheep to the high country.

Covered in dust and grime, with the smell of burning hide still lingering about the yards, Ken looked over the cattle.

'You know, Irwin, even if the mob did start from those half-wild brutes brought in from the Australian outback, we'd have some good stock here, with proper fences and pedigree sires.'

'And none of those cussed rabbits,' Irwin added.

'Did you know Joe's elder brother was sacked by Captain Kean down at Kaikoura for shooting a rabbit?'

'No!' Irwin had been long enough in the back country to realise what a pest rabbits were becoming.

'Fact,' said Ken. 'That idiot brought twelve silver-grey rabbits to Swincombe station, and let them loose. Not long after he sacked Joe's brother, he could see 100 of his precious silver-greys running in front of his horse.' Ken had to keep reminding himself — and Irwin and Mary — that if sheep and rabbits ruined Molesworth Moor Run it had nothing to do with him.

Now they were ready for the cattle drive to Hanmer, six weeks ahead of any possible storms. The heat of the very early autumn made droving slow and dusty, and the cattle were not quite up to the condition of the previous year. But Ken felt Elliott could have warned him about the transfer of the licence; he surely did not need to learn about it second-hand. More than 12 months would pass before Ken found that at least one of the mail deliveries had been swept away, the rider attempting to cross the Omaka in flood.

Alone in that vast acreage of mountains and rivers Mary looked forward to daybreak. She would be up and about, feeding the few hens that had somehow survived the bitter winter and the hot summer; the calf still running beside its mother preferred grass to milk; even if the milk was wasted on one person, she would set the pans for cream and ultimately butter. Straining it through muslin, she would once more regret that she had no pigs to guzzle the blue skim.

They had found looking after the sow and its progeny impossible. With no way of protecting the litter, Irwin had one morning buried ten miserable little runts, suffocated by the weight of the grunting mother. Of course Mary had known they might lose one or two, that also happened in Cornwall.

The whole litter destroyed. Her temper flew, she cursed the sow as Bill and Joe cursed their dogs.

When Irwin tried to pacify her, teasing her about her bullocky's language, she turned on him. What were they doing in this godforsaken hole? What use were they? 'And don't tell me I'm a good cook, I know that. I doubt any woman could do more with rabbits and flour, and that tough steer Ken couldn't get down from the tops in time to join the mob. But I'm tired of it all. I know you're saving money with your wages, but what for? Who's it for, if we freeze up here in the winter and swelter in the summer? And those gluttons of men. Why should I cook for them?'

Irwin pointed out that station hands usually had big appetites, the physical demands of their work were sometimes intense.

Mary would have none of it. Eventually the tempest subsided. For the first time Irwin began to suspect that his wife was not content with this back country life. She had worked so energetically and apparently so happily that he had not thought of looking beneath the facade. Ken was not the only frustrated person there. Another winter would be too much.

Yet he had not told Mary definitely that

122

they would leave with Ken, although he had quietly built that miner's cradle. He was wondering how she would react to his near return to that early life of a miner. He lacked words to explain how different prospecting for gold was from wresting tin ore from the depths of the earth.

It was in the southern twilight of the empty fields that Mary most noticed the isolation. The cattle were gone, the dogs, the horses. Even the wind was stilled, only the zonk of the Paradise Duck as a pair flew overhead, and the whistle of the Blue Duck later still.

Beady eyes peered from a corner. Despite the dogs and poison, rats still scampered into the kitchen as autumn advanced. Behind Barefell storm clouds piled up. The drovers and their mob must be well down the Acheron now, Mary thought; if only no rain fell in the Lake Tennyson area, they should be across the Clarence in a day or two. 'No use thinking about it,' she told herself despairingly, yet continued to reflect on the dangers of flooded rivers.

Towards morning the clash of thunder rolling round bare mountain faces woke her from an uneasy sleep. For three days rain fell solidly; below the whare the river was rising rapidly; no trees absorbed the sheets of water that tumbled down the slopes into the

Awatere, turning the torrent muddy with soil eroded from the sunburnt hillsides. She had stacked firewood in the kitchen, keeping the fire alight as the temperature fell, once again hot summer to freezing winter. Again they had left the droving too late, despite that six weeks' advance on the previous years. You could not predict the month of these storms, let alone the date.

Ah well, they knew she had plenty of stores to survive. God send Irwin did not try to get back to her early, before the others.

Each evening, once the storm had passed, found her listening for hoofbeats. It was impossible to forecast the men's return; perhaps the Clarence was in flood. Only the call of the ducks as they flew in their v-formation overhead in a quiet sunset. Perhaps tomorrow? Mary wished now she had accepted their offer of a horse to ride down to Polly at Langridge. If she gave into her loneliness and fear now, and decided to walk down tomorrow, Ken and Irwin might return the following day. It was too late to change her mind.

When at last the slow clop of hooves carried up the track, Mary was almost beside herself. Four horses, not much more than the size of calves from this distance, and the laden packhorses. She stoked up the fire before she flew to meet them, tearful with happiness.

'Never again,' she told Irwin that night. 'If there's a next time, I go with you. The rats can have it all to themselves.'

'Would you have been as lonely in Blenheim?' he asked kindly.

'Of course not. But you, you're not planning to stay here alone, are you? I'll stay, even here, with you. But I must ride along with you when you are going to be across those rivers for days at a time. Don't leave me alone here.'

'Ken has decided to leave, Mary. I'll go with him.'

'You said I. You meant both of us, didn't you?'

Mary was hurt; perhaps it was only a slip of the tongue, Irwin not thinking. 'Where'll we go, Irwin? Back to Blenheim? I'd like that.'

'We've decided we'll take up the Miner's Claim we registered, in the Wakamarina.'

'And you'll be a miner again? Oh, Irwin. We left Cornwall for you to get out of the mines. No, I'll stay on Molesworth with you. There's only the snow and the rivers. No mine workings to cave in. I've known of too many miners' widows.'

'My good woman,' Irwin said impatiently, 'you've the wrong idea altogether. Listen to

125

me. Mining for gold in most places isn't like the mining we know. I don't know why they call them miners. They pan for gold, work above ground anyway.'

'What d'you mean by pan for gold?'

'It's hard to explain, especially when you go on thinking of the mines you've seen. We work round the riverbed, washing the stones until we see gold settling in the bottom of the pan. It's easy.' (No word to Mary of back-breaking work with pick and shovel and cradle, Irwin had decided.)

Half-convinced, she said, 'I'll be with you, I'm glad to be going. So glad you said we'd take up the claim.'

'Those shanty-towns are no place for a woman like you, Mary.'

'But I've proved I can manage.'

'Yes, of course you have. I knew you could do it. What I'm trying to tell you is that the only women on the goldfields are usually . . . well, you might call them women of easy virtue. Ken is going with me. I want you to go on with your garden, make your home in the cottage. There'll be a little money now to spare for the fripperies you women like in a house.'

Before the first snowfall Mary was riding to the Acheron headwaters for the last time. An accomplished horsewoman now, she found the journey easy, and fast. Brown clouds as they threaded their way over the Saxton Saddle warned them to move quickly down the upper reaches of the Waihopai. It would have been very hard on their horses to ride through to Renwick Town in one day; and they lost a little time when Irwin, thinking about his incomplete cradle, drew Ken's attention to a dead sheep. 'A wool mat under the riffles at the bottom of the box,' he hinted.

The men reined in. Mary would come to no harm, ambling on that sure-footed mare towards the evening camp. Though the carcass had lain there some days, pecked by noisy keas and hawks, the wool was still firm on the skin. It took Ken only moments to remove as much woolly skin as Irwin needed, to trim out that precious piece that would hold all their gold.

They camped for this last night in the open, downstream of the Spray River junction, under the Devil's Backbone, the shadow of Tapuaenuku lost in the distance far behind the foothills.

If Mary was saddle-sore, she was unaware of it as the second long day brought them back to the cob cottage; no bullock-wagon this time, only the packhorses carrying the possessions they had taken to Molesworth.

9

Beaver Town had changed little more than its name, although soon it was to become the capital of Marlborough Province. The protracted arguments and the nonsensical election of two Provincial Superintendents, one in Picton and one in Blenheim, were over. The population had swollen in a few years from 300 to 3000; but many of the newcomers had joined the rush to the Wakamarina, as Ken and Irwin had learned on their earlier visit.

The town was still without roads and drains. The 'Board of Works' had no revenue, as its members, mainly landowners, objected to taxing themselves, especially for 'works' within the township.

Rumours floated back from Havelock that experienced diggers were leaving Deep Creek. The rush was over.

'We'll still head for that claim,' Ken told Irwin. 'Those miners leaving for the West Coast, that means more room for those who stay.'

'D'you think they'll have worked over our claim?'

'I don't think so, but we might have to shovel more gravel. The floods might have washed down a bit.'

'Floods there, too?'

'Floods everywhere in this province. We're lucky coming in later, it'll be easy to see where we should camp.'

Mary watched them ride off: the packhorse laden with stores, those rockers that had caused such anguish, canvas, tools and gleaming on top of the load a pan. How useful it would have been, she thought, to fill those greedy mouths at Molesworth. They had left Tapuaenuku, 'the footsteps of the rainbow god'. Would they find the pot of gold at the rainbow's end? She did not dare to mention that hope, the excitement she felt.

Ken and Irwin took the expedition quietly enough. On the surface it was just another job, as Ken had said, assessing the possibilities in a clinical mood. At worst he was sure his friend would make a little more out of the claim than his wages on a back country run. But underneath the veneer of calm acceptance, both men felt the lure of gold fever, the gamble with fortune and fate. They might strike it rich. Never once did they consciously admit that hope, even to each other.

The womenfolk, left behind like Mary, coped with families as they always had done, and now with fires and floods. They learned to row little dinghies down flooded streets to visit their friends in two-storey dwellings, or to live with them for a day or two if their own homes were single-storeyed in a ponding area.

It became a way of life.

Mary, still with that unspoken and grim determination to be a real pioneer wife, discovered in the midst of it all, with Irwin miles away beyond Havelock, that the longed for baby was on its way.

If she asked him, would he come back to work a claim at Onamaluta? she wondered. Though it was across the often-threatening Wairau River, it was not nearly so far away. But she would not write, she would not make that suggestion. He would have to ask Ken to read the letter, and from pride he would not like admitting his ignorance. She still puzzled about that. Figures were no trouble to him and he had gone to school. Perhaps he had been told as a young boy that reading was a waste of time; it would, however, be admitted that as a tin-miner he'd need at some stage to keep a tally.

Even if he did overcome his pride enough to ask Ken to read the letter, he would not reply. She would be no further ahead in hearing news of him. Living alone in

Blenheim was of course far less demanding than living at Molesworth in her husband's company and cooking for four men over that open fire, especially in those summer days of 80 degrees.

Mary, for the first time in her twenty odd years was blooming, aware of these first months of pregnancy that were such a delight. With no man to feed, no working clothes to wash, the days were almost her own. Every surface gleamed with home-made polish and elbow grease, the range was blackleaded, the sheen mirroring the face of its owner. No corner held a particle of dust. She had never needed to dig dirt out of the corners with a four inch-nail as she had at Molesworth. Before the rats so bothered her, in the early days she had thought she dug a dead mouse out of a corner; it was just thick dust and dirt that clung together in the shape of a tail-less mouse.

Then with everything gleaming she would leave the cob cottage to help Jean with the toddler, foreshadowed during that picnic on the riverbank. The other attraction there, for the seamstress Mary had been, was a treadle machine. From flour bags washed and bleached she could turn out rompers for Jean's baby, aprons for both of them. Scraps of material would turn into covers over layers

131

of old blankets or even sugar bags for warmth.

Neither she nor Jean lacked companionship and fun. All the congregations were involved in social gatherings as well as religious. The manse was now in Blenheim, not Renwick Town as it had been earlier. The church the Presbyterians had started to build had turned during a flood into a kind of Noah's Ark without animals; the frame, only just erected on plates, voyaged down the Omaka River until it stranded at the bridge. The Methodists who had met at Mrs Reid's house for the previous five years had built their church. The Roman Catholics moved into their new building a year or so later. A certain amount of rivalry was apparent in the head count at services, but not at socials, which could almost be described as ecumenical.

Sales of work organised by the women's groups allied to different churches would start with sewing-bees. It didn't matter which church they attended, Jean and Mary turned up at most sales, the money raised generally going to overseas missions but sometimes to church building funds.

There could be a threepenny raffle, though not at the Presbyterian or Methodist Sale of Work. There the patrons assessed the number of beans in a bottle or, if the butcher or one of the farmers had been kind, the weight of a side of mutton.

When committees noticed Mary's beautiful handwork, she was asked to edge special little frocks with lace. Any tricky sewing problem was referred to her. Lace-edged caps were a speciality; she even concocted bonnets for Jean and herself, shaped at the back to hold their neat buns. No-one stole hairpins here in Blenheim, Mary found.

Later, when the coming baby was beginning to show despite the ever-widened crinoline waist, wives of business men would give her oddments of fine tussore silk 'for the little one' and wincey for the gowns. The shopkeepers were kept busy; drapers' wives could find those inexpensive remnants for the Sale of Work and for their friends. They found Mary a charming woman, always ready to thread her needle for any dainty task. Those hard-worked pioneer hands could accomplish very fine work in daylight or by candle-light.

Alone, she would bend her head beside the candle, always the candle, to featherstitch long cuffs and bodices, or to whip a precious fragment of lace onto a boned collar. This first baby would not need to be dressed in old green serge cut from worn skirts, or black from the workaday blouses. Someone had given her that horrible magenta, she complained to Jean, but she would hide it in a drawer until it could become a duster.

Paddle-boats came upriver from the Wairau Bar; no longer did horses tow barges. The flour mill out towards Tuamarina provided flour for the housewives; they did not have to rely on the sometimes weevil-infested cargoes shipped to the port.

Mary hated weevils. Their fine silky strings, first sign of infestation, made her sick, especially now during her pregnancy. As for the crawling grubs in the meal, she would dash outside to vomit before she tried to sieve the flour and discard the wriggling bodies in the strainer.

Jean, very matter-of-fact, laughed at this squeamishness. 'There's worse things, and they'll cook. They do for meat and flavouring,' she teased once.

'I'm not sure if I don't hate those more than I hate rats,' Mary confessed.

'I'd rather have weevils than rats,' said Jean. 'At least weevils won't bite the baby.'

It was usual for a friend or neighbour to act as midwife; but some symptoms, not altogether common according to Jean, sent Mary to Dr Horne. At first she had thought him gruff and severe, mistaking that abrupt straightforward manner of his, until she

SHADOW OF THE MOUNTAIN

This is the story of Irwin and Mary Trelissick, who, over a century ago, sailed from Cornwall to begin a new life in New Zealand. They suffered a terrible journey and Mary swore she would never set foot on board a ship again. At first, they went to the Molesworth high country, where they endured the isolation and snows. Then they settled in Blenheim, where they had to contend with floods, arson, epidemics and earthquakes. Sometimes patience was short and tempers flared in the tiny cob cottage which they built themselves and in which they reared their seven children.

Books by Iris Nolan
Published by The House of Ulverscroft:

BELLS FOR CAROLINE

realised his kindness. He knew how she longed for this first child; he was determined it should survive, as so often babies in similar cases without expert attention did not.

Young James took his time about arriving. Sometime in the middle of the protracted labour Mary clutched Jean's hand to groan: 'I'll never want another baby.'

Old Dr Horne patted her shoulder. 'You'll forget this, you'll see. I'll help you through the next births, too.'

Sadly, by the time Jamie was toddling blissfully into mischief, Dr Horne had perished in the first of the township fires where arson was suspected.

10

As Ken and Irwin had discussed, many of the tents had vanished at the tail end of the rush. Some of the original camps had been carried away by floods in the Wakamarina. Other diggers, who had crowded the tracks when Rutland, Harrison and Wilson had announced their discovery of payable gold in Mountain Camp Creek, had travelled to the West Coast for richer rewards. The New South Wales Bank agency had closed; the Bank of New Zealand had been appointed Gold Receiver.

The gaps between the tents were squalid and muddy, with rubbish where it had fallen as they took down their shelters. A mist of despondency hung over the few wives who had followed their husbands onto the goldfield. The women of easy virtue to whom Irwin had referred were in the minority, now at least; they had stayed with the free-and-easy grog shops in Havelock, or followed the hard-living groups to new fields. Irwin hoped Mary would not ever meet any of the faithful wives; she would be sure she could have joined him in Canvastown, and would be angry about being left behind.

A solitary prospector — hatters they were called — his camp far apart from the tattered village, took his pipe from his mouth to wave towards the more crowded areas: 'Anywhere over there, gentlemen, I won't have no neighbours.'

Ken asked him how he was doing.

'A little bit better than tucker,' the hatter said. 'You'll be all right, the riff-raff's gone to the Buller. Grogging all night and fighting all day, some of them.'

'We were told it was a law-abiding field,' said Irwin.

'It was, once the Mining Registrar showed them his revolvers,' the old man answered. 'He slept with two under his pillow.'

However, when Ken asked him the best way to find gold he was abrupt. 'You find out for yourself,' the prospector said. 'You've got a claim, you work it.'

Warned by signs of previous floods, Ken also selected a site without neighbours. He had bought good quality canvas to roof their tent, not much more than a shelter but much ahead of their tattered roof of high country experience. Others here in Canvastown were worse off; a blanket flung over manuka poles provided their only roofing.

With the exodus of the rougher element the

camp was normally quiet; the odd quarrel would erupt into fisticuffs, but the days of the shouting, grog-induced free-for-all had vanished. Fighting now was more for enjoyment, to relieve the boredom, not that determined effort to take over a claim or knock someone out of the way. Belongings as well as claims were much safer. But the cradle, when complete, would need to be carried from the riverbank up to the camp each night. Sudden flood might well take it away as quickly as the most diligent plunderer.

While Irwin was putting the cradle together — he had finally agreed with Ken that it was too unwieldy completed to be transported, although they had taken a packhorse as far as Havelock — the old hatter left his hut to watch the carpentry more closely. First one then another from the main camp joined him, like cattle closing in on someone walking through a paddock.

Irwin suddenly became aware of the onlookers. 'What's the matter?' he asked. 'If you were those steers on Molesworth, I'd set a dog onto you.'

A few sniggered.

But the hatter, ever the gentleman, removed his pipe from his mouth. 'There's nought the matter. But you've brought me away from my camp, to be with people.'

'That's the first time since we've been here,' said one of the diggers.

'Why?' Irwin queried, bewildered. 'I'm making the cradle the right way, aren't I?'

'Very good it is,' admitted the hatter. 'Yet your rockers are crafted like furniture, and that rusty piece of iron is no match for the rest of your work.'

'And,' added another, 'that sheepskin mat stinks. Why didn't you buy a bit of matting somewhere?'

'We sorted it all out in the back country,' Irwin said.

'There's always stores near a goldfield. Surely there was one near you?'

Irwin glanced at the wordless Ken; these prospectors must imagine they were experienced diggers. To the enquirer he said, 'Not so far away. About three days on horseback.' He finished putting the cradle together in utter silence.

Meanwhile Ken tried panning. He loaded the pan, as he saw others doing, with paydirt, washed it thoroughly by scrabbling his fingers through it, then went on with the laborious task of swirling and tipping, each time emptying out only a few of the larger pieces of gravel. By then he was convinced that, failing a sluice, and with two working together, the cradle should be more profitable. Once the sheepskin mat was well-covered with fine sand and gold-dust (if any), panning, the final washing up, would not be so demanding.

First the top gravel had to be removed, before they could load the cradle, one then heaving shovelfuls of paydirt onto the rusty iron, the other scooping up water with a battered tin and rocking the cradle backwards and forwards vigorously. The bigger pieces of gravel were cleared off the hopper before the next loading. Daylight till dark they worked with the sand and gold in the sheepskin between the riffles, panned towards the end of a long afternoon.

In spite of the high, tight-fitting Nugget Boots bought in Blenheim, where the shops vied with Nelson in stocking diggers' outfits, Ken and Irwin were always wet and cold. They wore the uniform of the goldfields, flannel shirts, moleskin trousers and tall wide-awake hats; their companions now were mostly well-to-do working class, often well-connected, men already on the make.

Ken laughed so good-naturedly at the jeers — he was a toff, a dude (from a Californian) — that the barracking soon stopped. Few went to the lengths he did, to hold on to some vestiges of civilisation in the ragged encampment. At Molesworth he had always changed for the evening meal although again it would be stewed rabbit. Irwin, noticing, as he rarely did, what went on around him, had followed suit. Here, round a smoky fire that served also to keep the hordes of mosquitoes away, they would crouch, bent-kneed, after a wash in the cold river, in clean clothing not often dry. The next day they would be back in the wet and muddy outfit of today's labour.

'Those mosquitoes don't seem to be wearing grey gumboots,' Ken commented one evening when the smoke did not keep them at bay, 'they must be a different species.'

Irwin was bewildered. Mosquitoes, in gumboots? 'I don't understand,' he said.

Ken explained without a smile. 'In the first rush the mosquitoes used to arrive in clouds. They darkened the sun, the diggers expected thunder until they got used to it. One day they fastened onto old Charlie's blanket. He hadn't washed it for years, so it smelt human to those hungry mossies. They took it away with them when they flew off. They've all worn grey boots ever since.'

The men were always careful to show only a poker-face round the shantytown, like all the other diggers. The story of those 30 claim jumpers lingered, without sympathy, for

Moffit 'shouldn't have been such a blabber-mouthed fool,' they said. Every word warned the two friends to keep quiet about any good find they might have. Ears around the open tent precluded any discussion or display of satisfaction about a good day's yield.

Days when Irwin set off for Nelson through Havelock, the Maungatapu and the Maitai, Ken worked the cradle for half the day; then, after panning what had collected between the riffles, he would prospect upriver, beyond any marked claims. Their own 20 by 30 foot claim he would leave each half-day until Irwin's return almost a week later. Both regretted that the bank agencies in Deep Creek and Havelock had closed when the Bank of New Zealand was appointed Gold Receiver. Carrying gold was a time-consuming and risky business, especially alone. They discussed the question, but it seemed wise for one or the other to remain near the campsite. They were fortunate their claim was so far undisturbed. Sleazy characters had appeared and disappeared again, haunting the field to discover where riches might lie; the faces suggested that force or murder might not be beyond the strangers.

Twice in the intervals of panning Ken found tiny nuggets, not worth a fortune but better than dust. Like the old prospector they fared 'a little bit better than tucker'. But as the days went on, with barely enough gold dust to encourage them to try again, wet from the rain, the river and the overhanging beech trees, it became just another job — a horny-handed, back-breaking job with no great reward.

Irwin's trips became less frequent, and it was rarely that he carried more than 20 sovereigns' worth at a time, depending on the assay between 55 and 60 ounces at ruling rates.

They would find a half-ounce nugget; then, as if to keep the record straight, days would end with only sand in the riffles and hardly a gleam of gold. Carefully they worked over every square foot of the claim. They wondered if they had shovelled enough gravel to get down to the paydirt. Were they going deep enough for a decent find?

'There's not a soul we can ask about it,' Ken said, as they discussed the subject quietly after the evening meal. 'Either we'll be the butt of the camp — we've enough to put up with now — or they'll tell us we've cut the claim out.'

'And the minute we turn our backs,' Irwin finished for him, 'That greasy Californian'll jump the claim along with his mates.'

'I've noticed them,' said Ken. 'You never

see them working anywhere. But they're off to Havelock for a day or two, then come back loaded with grog and stores.'

'Wonder what they're up to?'

'Better not to know, I think, Irwin.'

'You're right there, find out too much and they'd run us out of the place.'

It was not a comfortable feeling. At least the majority of the diggers were hard-working (decent God-fearing people, said Irwin) and the stealthy possible claim jumpers remained quiet. The mining registrar kept his eyes open for probable trouble-makers; the presence of an occasional policeman on the field showed clearly that robbery would not be tolerated there, as it had been on some of the lawless Otago fields.

After a particularly fruitless day, Ken asked, 'D'you think we'd do better out of washing our shirts in the river, rather than panning?' The story of Elizabeth Pope's shirts and the first gold from Wakamarina had not been forgotten.

Perhaps that reminded Irwin of the wife he had left behind in Blenheim. Unlike the fancy free Ken, he had someone dependent on him. They were still finding some gold, but not enough to keep them both earning a good living. Diggers were combining to build sluices, sharing claims and the gold. The tents were fewer in number, the grumblers legion. Irwin gave up. Ken stayed on in Canvastown, but their unacknowledged hope of a rich strike had vanished, though others might be finding the occasional nugget.

11

Dirty and unkempt and with bloodshot eyes, Irwin staggered into the cob cottage. Greeting him with affection, his wife was amazed and hurt when he put her aside, none too gently. Jamie hiding behind his mother's skirt, cried at the sight of this strange rough man.

Putting the iron tub in front of the range, Mary hastened to fill it with hot water from the kettle, soap and towel beside it. While she pacified Jamie, Irwin dropped his filthy wet clothes on the floor. A meal was on the table for him by the time he had bathed and dressed.

'I'd like to let Ken know about the Pelorus River,' he told Mary. 'There's only two wires at the crossing. Miners on the bank yelled that the current was too strong, they said later, but I didn't hear them. I did get across, but the water was up to my neck. I'd have been a goner if they hadn't been there.'

Mary was horrified. 'Did they have to jump in to rescue you?'

'No, I got to the other bank. But they tell me I collapsed there, still half in the water. They dragged me up to their hut, stripped me

146

and put me into one of their bunks. They kept me there two days, and me worrying about the gold I was carrying for the bank in Nelson.'

'They took it, I suppose.'

'No, they didn't touch it, must have known it was there, too. They wouldn't even let me pay for the tucker I'd eaten, so I backpacked a hunk of meat, and flour — they made a real good damper, better than Ken or me — and sugar and tea. Left it with them on my way home.'

'They'd be pleased,' Mary said.

'Well, they saved my life. Now I'm dry, warm, clean and fed, where's that little lad I saw? Word got through to the camp that I had a son.'

It took patient coaxing by both parents to bring Jamie out of his corner behind his mother's rocking-chair. It took longer for him to allow the big silent man to pick him up. After a few days, though, he would trot round after his father.

When her little son was quiet, Mary expected mischief.

'Whatever you're doing, don't,' became a constant and much-favoured command.

About to look for him one morning, she peered through the diamond-paned window. He was not into mischief, far from it. About three paces behind his father, he solemnly tried to stretch his short legs to fit his father's footsteps. Hands in his pockets, just like father, he had an old clay pipe belonging to Irwin hanging from his mouth, just like father.

What would her husband do about that? Jamie had been told never to touch those pipes; they might burn him if the bowl was hot from recent use.

But when Irwin turned on his heel as he reached the fence at the end of the path, suddenly faced with a miniature edition of himself he shouted with laughter. He swung the boy into his arms, tossed him in the air, Jamie chortling with glee.

Not very good for discipline, Mary knew, but how glorious to see them such friends, and her husband so relaxed.

Aunt May's last and only generous gesture made a difference as well. Dying, she had bequeathed the freehold of the ten acres near Renwick Town to her nephew. Though the wilderness was still uncleared, it might produce food for the family though it could never have provided an income. Surely hard work could make something out of that ten acres?

Irwin had ignored the allotment when a monetary return was expected. That almost impossible task would have taken years. Now it was in his name he was not happy about leaving it in the rough. Besides, there was some talk in town that owners would be fined for failing to cut their gorse hedges. How would he get on in that case, with golden bloom and prickly stem rampant amongst matagouri, manuka, toi-toi and flax?

The period spent on the goldfield had changed her husband, Mary told Jean, in one of those rare sessions when she felt disloyal. She was concerned she had to talk to someone although she felt no-one could help. He would disappear, morose, for hours at a time between odd jobs. No permanent carpentering was available. Mary never knew where he was. At home he would ignore Jamie whom he had seemed to love. He had nothing to say to his wife, neither praise nor blame. Sometimes she wished he would be angry with her, just for the sake of conversation. She had spent so many months alone; she was little better off with Irwin in the house.

Jean tried to comfort her. 'Most men get like that between jobs, Mary. Take no notice. At least our husbands don't knock us about, like that stupid Arthur and his chatterbox of a wife. He told Tom that's the only way he can shut her up.'

'I think I'd almost rather Irwin did that instead of treating me like a log of firewood.'

Refusing to take Mary seriously, her friend laughed. 'He doesn't treat you like a log, Mary, he doesn't throw you on the fire!'

When the little steamers came up the river his wife knew where to find him; he would always be there, sometimes stevedoring with the others. Did he miss the sea? she wondered, or was life too full of disappointments? Hard work and being wet and cold had never bothered him before. He did not mention life in Canvastown; had the experiences there something to do with this almost unknown husband? If he longed for those ships and the sea, why not tell her?

Tiny ships, 18 to 40 tons, were used in the river trade: the *Mary* on which they had embarked in Port Underwood, the *Rapid* (she often was not), the *Necromancer*, always known as 'Old Nick' and known just as well for failing to respond to the wheel. The schooner *Alert*, carrying more cargo than the others, might be away for six weeks sailing to Port Nicholson and back. The paddle steamer *Lyttelton*, the first of the steam traders, was a constant visitor. Widened, lengthened and deepened, she was a household word, distant at least two days' sailing from the port from which she took her name.

Soon the whole town, including those as far from the river as the Trelissicks, would know when the larger schooners were coming upriver. The tug *Osprey*, a barge fitted with a portable engine, would puff up the Opawa River. Not only did the residents of Blenheim hear its efforts; 'Puffing Billy' could be heard all over the Wairau.

Ships meant something to Irwin, ships and water if not the sea. Perhaps, unaware in his conscious mind, he regretted the salt air of his younger days at home on the shores of the Helford estuary; he, like his wife, had no real wish to be involved in mining, that was simply the work that offered in his youth. Just as he had been thrust by circumstances into the tin mines, so he had pushed himself into working the land at Renwick Town without much hope of success, no heart in his efforts. The long voyage could have been the incentive to emigrate; Mary and Irwin were far apart in this respect.

Old Annie, slatternly, seldom without a black eye from her drunken lout of a husband was far more relaxed than either of the Trelissicks. She often dropped in on Mary, sure of a welcome and hot scones and tea, and of her hostess's understanding. Annie was fond of gin; she found her escape route in that bottle.

Mary had no difficulty with her chores, though the demanding twins, recent addition to the family, kept her busy. Molesworth had been a much more irksome taskmaster. Jamie's pranks, usually the result of an enquiring mind, she dealt with by the customary slap over the ears.

In rare happy moments Irwin would delight in the pretty little girls, Margaret and Jeanie. Then Jamie could put his chubby hand in the calloused big one and toddle into the shops, or up to the Taylor River, quietly watching his father while he fished for brown trout. Irwin usually brought home enough for a meal.

Suddenly the children would be a nuisance to the silent man, a brown bear Mary would call him, trying to cajole him out of the morose mood. He never lifted a hand to wife or children, just retreated. Often Mary would think an outburst of temper would be preferable to these inexplicable silences. No use asking him the cause. He would not — perhaps could not — answer.

Light-hearted and cheerful still, she could take no part in the dances, the gatherings where a husband or partner was essential for the matrons. Despite the constant grind, Mary, not much over five feet, had filled out; her friends referred to her as well-built. Irwin became gaunt and stooped. She fed him well, but could not, with all the will in the world, turn him into a contented man.

Her duty she did willingly, marriage was a duty. The couple rarely argued; mutual respect there was, and a tepid affection. Had she ever experienced love, that emotion of poetry and passion? Her feelings had been rather those of respect and admiration for a man who had rescued her from a dull, sad and unpromising future.

What of Irwin? Love? Or respect and a kind of adoration in the quality of life and personality that was Mary, so far above his status that he would not ever have expected to be able to ally himself with it. Neither could answer those queries. Luckily Mary was far too busy to mull over them.

Rumour whispered frighteningly in the town. The Kelly gang had come north from the Otago goldfields. Men looked to their firearms, discussed forming a vigilante group; the Banks took extra safeguards.

When Jean went round to the Trelissick home with Tom, he jovially clapped Irwin on the back. 'Just as well you're home, Irwin. Mary'd be frantic with worry. She'd be thinking about you over the hills. And she'd probably be concerned about being alone with the youngsters here.'

'The Kelly gang, you mean?' Irwin asked. 'Rumour, they won't come here. Those missing men were drowned in the Rai Valley. I nearly drowned in the Pelorus myself.'

'They weren't drowned. Flett, the Nelson constable, has found the bodies.'

'Murdered?' gasped Mary.

'Any word of who they are?' Irwin asked anxiously.

'No. — Guess there's not been enough time,' Tom answered. 'They'd be from Onamaluta or Wakamarina, for sure. You were up at Canvastown, you might know them.'

'Yes' was the abrupt reply.

'Maybe they'll catch that damned murdering Kelly gang now,' said Tom viciously. 'I'd like to lynch the thieving rogues myself.'

'It's not the gang I'm thinking about,' Mary broke in, 'it's the poor wives.'

'Or friends,' Irwin muttered quietly. 'One of them might not be married.'

She began to realise what he was thinking. 'Not Ken?' she asked, incredulously. 'He wouldn't be taking gold to Nelson.'

'I don't know,' replied Irwin. 'That's the way we used to go, but usually alone, not with other fellows. That's why I was crossing the Pelorus before I came home, taking our dust to Nelson. I'd told Ken I'd come home from there. He could work the claim and keep what he found.'

'You're only guessing the worst,' objected Tom. 'No reason why it should be Ken. Rumour says none of them had any gold, they were only travellers, surveyors or some such.'

'Well, they wouldn't have any gold after Sullivan and Levy had a go at them, would they?'

'All right, all right, Irwin. How about waiting to hear more before the women start finding your blacks to wear to Ken's funeral?'

Jean, usually placid, flared up. 'Tom, don't joke about it.'

'Sorry, my dear,' he said. 'But there's dozens of fossickers out there, anyway. After all, Irwin, you got through safely, how many times? And all the others?'

'You're right, old friend,' Irwin agreed, calming down. 'Can't do a bit of good looking for trouble.'

'We'll have a beer down at the pub,' said Tom. 'Word'll come through any time now.'

The two women regarded one another with resignation. Ah well, they would boil the kettle, again, and look after the children, again, and wait for news, as women always have done.

Within a day or two the couples learned to their relief that Ken was not among the murdered trio, none of them known to Irwin.

It was a shocking crime, and the townsfolk rejoiced with all New Zealanders when at last 'the Kelly gang', who had terrorised the Otago goldfields for some time, were convicted and executed for the Maungatapu murders.

Then Irwin crossed the Wairau for three or four weeks, still hoping to make a fortune from alluvial gold at Onamaluta. Discovered about the same time as the Wakamarina fields, it had been the scene of a minor rush. But the more experienced men soon realised that machinery was needed rather than pick, shovel and pan, with a stream nearby.

Those with ties with Wellington celebrated when the Cook Strait cable was laid, with its terminal at Whites Bay. It would be years before the lonely telegraph staff stationed there would move to Blenheim.

That meant nothing to Mary. Here in this tiny cob cottage was all she valued, and all she wanted when Irwin was home. What if the 'Long Drop', like so many others in the town, affected the quality of water in slow-running drains and stagnant pools? To her, a water-table was a ditch beside the road. What if she heated water in unwieldy iron cauldrons on the stove, and washed in a galvanised iron tub? She had to avoid one or two rust spots now appearing inside the tub, for all her care. Jean told her salts of lemon solved the problem of rust spots on linen; but that was a trifling extra Mary could not afford.

Happy-go-lucky Tom Jones had installed a water boiler beside his wife's range; Mary would not ask Irwin if he could afford one for her. Besides, when Jean needed a very hot oven for her feathery scones, sometimes the water boiled out, all rusty. More trouble than enough, Mary decided. Essential groceries only were all she would request on her husband's return.

How much gold or money, what he did with it: these were no questions for a Victorian wife, even if she was a pioneer. The family might cost more to feed, but their clothes descended, mended, made over, cut down from one to the other, from Jamie to the twins unless the garments were too boyish, and from them to baby Michael.

As the girls grew, they found themselves in dark clothing often too warm for the sunny Blenheim climate. Mary would have discarded a voluminous skirt, to cut from it two little frocks. Jean would fly in sometimes with garments her older children would no longer wear, or the younger one would not. How did she buy material? and even made-up dresses for herself? Mary vaguely wondered. Yet she loved completing the tiny clothes, especially when her fine needlework could be used to decorate, or when there was reason to visit Jean, to borrow her treadle machine. Whether tongues wagged faster than the machine needle no-one would ever ask. It was a happy time, except for Irwin being away. And maybe he would return more like the man she had known before — before Molesworth? Or before Renwick Town? He had been relaxed, happy on the voyage except when she was sick. That was the best time of their marriage for her husband, she considered, the future was not in his hands.

12

Irwin was still at Onamaluta when heavy rain curtained the Wither Hills, warning the townspeople to remove themselves and their belongings to higher ground. Jean and Tom came round to collect Mary and the children. Their concern was disregarded. Wee Jeanie had a cold, she could not be taken from her warm bed out into the bitter rain, her mother stated.

'Mary,' said Jean, 'you'll have to leave here, they say this might be the worst ever. That warm spell melted the snow round Lake Rotoiti. And the Wairau was running a banker before the rain started.'

'What's that got to do with the Opawa?' Mary snapped, her hostility surprising her friend. 'I only hope Irwin didn't leave Onamaluta yesterday, he'd have to cross the Wairau. Don't tell me about it. Anyway, it's cold enough to stop the snow melting.'

Tom looked away. He had heard that two men had been drowned, hit by rearing logs on the crossing. 'If the snow melts round Tophouse,' he tried to explain, 'there's bound to have been a thaw on all those peaks east of the St Arnaud, that means a flood in the Waihopai, backing up against the Wairau. And Omaka and Opawa floodwaters are held back by the swollen Wairau already.'

'Please come with us now,' Jean pleaded. 'We'll wrap my little god-daughter up warmly.'

'You go, Jean; Irwin showed me how you're in that loop of the Taylor. It's good of you both to think of us,' Mary replied, more friendly, more the gracious woman they expected to find. 'I'm sure we're above the flood level. Irwin would wonder where his family had gone when he arrives.'

Again that troubled glance, unobserved, between Tom and his wife.

'Look, we can carry the children over the ditches if we go now. We're all welcome on the second floor of the Marlborough. We don't want to have to collect you later in the dinghy.'

'It won't come to that,' argued Mary obstinately, forgetting that her friends had more experience of Beaver Town than she. 'You go. We'll be all right, and Irwin will get here presently.'

How could Tom point out that Irwin would have reached the town by now? If he had left the diggings early enough and if — that was his major concern — he had crossed the Wairau safely.

No amount of persuasion could change Mary's mind. The ditches were overflowing, the apologies for roads already awash. Tom had his own family to consider. Soon they would not be able to splash to safety, with the muddy current getting stronger every minute. He certainly could not explain why he was afraid Irwin could not reach his family in time to help them. All he could do was to ask the nearest volunteer fire brigadesman to keep an eye on the cottage. Surely Mary would be prepared to abandon the dwelling before water began to climb up the walls, long before it reached the low windowsills. She would not roost in the attic with all those children? Suppose the roof collapsed? Unlikely, but cob buildings had been destroyed on the Plain. It didn't bear thinking of.

Hours of rain passed slowly enough. Muddy water gleamed among the lower stretch of toi-tois and flax that separated her from the town-ship. Behind the cottage, not very far distant, the Omaka was spreading across the swamp. Presently the fence was covered; debris that had floated quietly past on the road began to surge against the outbuildings. Mary had piled all the movable articles on the table, with Michael's cradle in the middle. Jamie and Margaret cuddled beside her while she nursed Jeanie, hot and fretful.

'What a fool I am,' Mary muttered. 'Of course Irwin wouldn't get here. He's safe in the hills at Onomaluta. I wonder if he cares about us at all?' That was an unfair comment, she knew; yet all her miseries were coming to the surface, fury bubbling up under that placid surface she showed to Irwin and her friends. She was tired of battling with fate alone, while another woman's husband had to see if she could manage.

The rivers were joining in angry torrents in the murky twilight, muddy seething threats carrying trees and the corpses of livestock.

Would the door Irwin had built keep the water out? The children were crowding together now on the table-top, Margaret crying with fright, Jeanie very hot in fever, struggling to push off the wrappings. Jamie, white-faced but proud of being the man of the family, was rocking Michael.

'Gently,' said their mother. 'He's asleep, Jamie, don't wake him. Margaret, stop crying. Look at Jeanie, how good she is.'

Water up the outer wall now, gurgling under that well-fitted door. Was their home wattle and daub? Mary had forgotten the decision to build a rammed earth cottage. Did it matter? Would the walls withstand this flood, or would the dwelling wash away altogether? Could she carry Margaret up the ladder to the attic? What she should have done, she admonished herself, did not matter. What to do now was important. She would have to decide about the attic before the floor was covered with such a depth of water that Jamie, as well as the girls would have to be carried to safety, above the surging flood. Or should she wait here for a rescue which the men would try to make? Irwin was stronger, taller; and he was away when she needed him, as he so often had been. Somehow he had disregarded her, sure she could manage; he had forgotten the frail and cared-for manager's daughter. In those minutes of peril Mary decided that she had taken on too much. Her own fault, she knew; she had wanted to be a worthy pioneer wife and she had proved herself. But at what a cost! She would have been weeping like the children had they not needed her support. She should have been another Auntie May, she thought, leaning on her husband, not trying all the time to be self-reliant.

Minutes dragged into hours in her mind. The relentless ticking of the clock on the mantel told her that little more than an hour had passed while they watched the swirling tree-trunks. One banged against the house wall. It trembled slightly; the water, as she could see, was lapping the low sills. Why hadn't she listened to Tom and Jean? They had lived through all those earlier floods, Mary recollected now — too late. And what had been the use of waiting for Irwin? They could wait forever. Holding tightly to her control for the sake of the children clutching her hands, she shivered. It was getting dark earlier than ever with the lowering skies and curtains of rain. Could they bring a dray to rescue the family? That question was answered as the carcass of a bullock was swept by where Tom and Jean had waded to safety.

Then in the distance she saw one of the whaleboats from the Opawa wharf. Four men were pulling strongly on their oars, sending the craft at a long diagonal across the current. Already six women with their crying children huddled together on the thwarts.

'More fools like me,' Mary whispered to herself. 'How can we all fit in? It looks as though they can't make another trip.'

She was unaware of the danger threatened by rearing tree-trunks, fended off by the oarsmen. Tom, pulling strongly, was thinking about Irwin's paling fence. How deep was the water? Would the boat, laden as it was, float over it? Should he try to swim in that wet thickness, to lighten the load?

This suggestion was smartly discounted by the others. 'You'd never manage it, Tom,' said one. 'Besides, we need you. We'll have to risk going aground.'

Tom was glad he had told Irwin that a fence to keep driven cattle off the garden could be much less than six feet high.

The rowers held their oars against the current while Tom scrambled into the flooded room. Jamie, then Margaret and baby Michael were handed across to the over-crowded boat. How they would cope Tom had no idea; there had been little enough freeboard for safety earlier. He grabbed an enamel jug from the bench to serve as another bailer. The water swirled in, more than knee-deep, as he steadied Mary, with Jeanie held high in her arms, across the floor to the doorstep where the boat waited.

By the time all were aboard, it was loaded to the gunwales. When one of the boys, excited rather than frightened, leaned over to grab a wooden toy floating by, a tiny ripple came into the boat before his mother dragged him back from the side. The jug as well as the proper bailer with which they were equipped was brought into action. The steady rain added to the pool sloshing about in the bilges.

It was quite dark in the hotel entrance when finally, exhausted and silent, they stepped into the muddy layer which already reached the fourth stair.

Again the children, the last to be rescued, had to be carried by the tired men. From upstairs those in safety there had seen the whaler approach; willing hands helped the drenched passengers upstairs. Jean rushed to take her namesake, while Mary stumbled up the rest of the flight into the crowded room. Stripping off sodden clothes in bathrooms festooned with sou'westers and oilskins, the new arrivals wrapped themselves in blankets stencilled 'The Marlborough Hotel'.

No-one asked: 'Why didn't you leave your home earlier?'

That comment need not be made. They would all leave well ahead of time when floods next menaced their homes.

During the day before the water dropped enough for most to go home to clean up once again, Mary heard that three men, as yet unnamed, had been drowned trying to cross from the north bank of the Wairau.

'Why didn't the fools go to Langley Dale?' asked one stranger. 'That's so isolated there's almost a full township round the homestead.'

'Or down to Tuamarina?' a beery voice suggested.

'Floods of beer within and water without,' someone murmured.

'What's that?' demanded the beery one. 'Put yer dooks up,' he ordered threateningly.

'My good man,' said the other, 'We've more to do than fight.'

'Yes, you have,' snapped Mary. 'Shut up and look if the flood level's dropping. Stop making such a damned row when the children are trying to sleep on the floor.'

Tom and Jean were astounded. Quietly spoken Mary, who would think twice before she offered an opinion in the company of her friends, using some of old Annie's language.

'Tha'sh right,' Annie was there, too, no more bedraggled than usual, but happier than others, with less to lose and a supply of her beloved gin handy. 'Give it to them, dearie, the silly old buggers. Where's your man, anyhow?'

'Sh.' Tom whispered. 'We don't know if he was one of those idiots who tried to cross the Wairau in flood.'

Annie grunted and subsided. She might be and was rough, but she had the inborn kindliness and tact of a gentlewoman.

Home again, in the stale-smelling slime of the flooded cottage. Everyone with their

167

hands full, trying to scrub furniture and floors, dry clothing, rebuild from debris the outhouses carried off by the rivers. As the sun warmed the receding pools, the stench of drowned animals overwhelmed the sourness of the swamps.

Mary, tired out, choked with the thought of these young children dependent on her alone. Where was the man of the house when he was needed? She had accepted the fact that he was unable to join them earlier because of the Wairau levels; she was quite sure he had not even started out when the rains began. He hadn't died, he should be here instead of avoiding his duties. Her fear and anger stifled her usual honesty; Irwin was not there because he was trying to provide for them. But he should provide for a young family by living at home.

A few days later Irwin reappeared, unconcerned about his family's survival. He was comfortably sure his wife would cope; indeed he was cross that she had refused to leave home earlier, when, unfortunately for Mary, he heard from Tom about his first visit to persuade the family to leave the cottage.

Jean was angry. 'Doesn't Mary have enough to put up with, Tom, without putting her in the wrong?'

'Well, Irwin asked me why I had to get

them out by boat. He's in a sour mood, too. He accused me of forgetting about them.'

Placid Jean accepted her husband's excuse. That little domestic rift was soon mended.

The atmosphere at Trelissick's, however, was far from comfortable. Not that Irwin and Mary quarrelled openly; it might have been better if they had. Mary carried on with the cleaning up; she had set out to be a pioneer, and she would be successful. Irwin was aware, underneath, that she felt he had ignored the family's crisis; he had brought home no gold; and there was no topsoil at all on the ten acres at Renwick Town. The flood had carried it out to sea together with the few plantings he had managed, and everything from the Langleydale flats — fences, pasture, topsoil, stock they had not had time to muster to higher ground. Most of the level land had been washed out, deposited on the Wairau Bar, it seemed; Cloudy Bay carried that muddy film seawards for days with ebbing tides. The pioneers on the Plain had weathered over a decade of such troubles, and had enough behind them to survive, replant and fence the flats.

But Irwin, how could he start again? The waters that eroded the topsoil revealed boulder-strewn clay. What could grow in those conditions? And how much would the next flood destroy? Aunt May's bequest was more of a burden than her earlier penny-pinching suggestions.

Worse was to come. Diphtheria raged through the town of water-logged shacks and cottages. The day the Presbyterian minister, dying from the disease, was buried, wee Jeanie was lowered into a tiny grave.

Mary tried humbly to thank God that diphtheria had not touched the rest of the family. In some households all the children had been infected, and many of them perished, especially in the lower-lying areas where the advice to boil even tank water was disregarded. One desolate couple had trudged south, abandoning everything, after they had buried their six children, the youngest a babe of six months.

Perhaps Jeanie's fever had lowered her resistance. Or was the diphtheria germ already about in conditions of poor sanitation, before the flood and the crowding of refugees spread it so rapidly?

There was nothing to do but carry on. Husband and wife broke silence to discuss where they could go. Again to Molesworth, at least out of reach of flooded homes and epidemics? With Jamie and Margaret, the now toddling Michael, and another baby, Mary realised, on the way? Irwin thought a new baby would replace lost Jeanie, so far he was from understanding Mary.

'Lost Jeanie will grow along with Margaret,' she said to Jean. 'No child is ever lost completely. Don't fathers feel like that?'

Jean could not answer. All her brood had survived, despite some infection; yet she felt fairly sure that Tom would have understood, had one of their children died.

13

Labouring jobs were plentiful in the aftermath of the flood, but Irwin was able to find work he enjoyed. Mr Sinclair was building the first wooden house in Blenheim, much to the amazement of the many who were sure rammed earth was the only proper material. They, from the Old Country, had not yet allowed for Blenheim's better climate, with hard frosts followed by brilliantly sunny days.

Sinclair's house would not float away like the church; the owner had selected rising ground well clear of any flood, 'unless we ever need Noah and his ark,' he commented, not short of a sense of humour. With its three dormer windows, the dwelling set a style different from the ragged collection of shacks and cottages in the swampland, where raupo encouraged stagnant pools.

The borough was gazetted, with the roadless, drainless area under its control. Tom Jones thought they might manage to prevent some of the most severe flooding. But many of the streets were still the property of the subdividers, like Messrs. Fell and Seymour; efforts to lessen the danger in one direction often led to accusations that other parts would become lakes.

In some ways it was such a town of the Wild West that one of the first by-laws prohibited riding at a furious pace in the streets. Mary was grateful; going to school one day Jamie had almost become one of the victims. Similar legal prohibitions abated some nuisances, others flourished despite local complaints. Wool-washing, which added to the distinctive odours of the swamps, continued in Arthur Street, despite outcries for its removal.

Irwin came home with the cheerful rumour that flooding would soon be a thing of the past. 'They' were going to drain a swamp behind that street of the wool-washers, and drain the Taylor River into the Omaka. One way and another Lock-up Creek became a new name in the records and in conversation.

Once Mr Sinclair's house was completed, Irwin was again looking for a job. He wanted to continue as a carpenter; perhaps timbering would be used for protective works, to prevent the Opawa and Omaka overflowing. But he would not handle the boulders that on the Wairau Plain were the cheapest form of groyne or embankment.

Bridges made life easier, though it was a matter of using the punt when the Grove

Road Bridge was out of action, closed so frequently by flood waters that it was considered tidal.

Progress was signalled by small outings, excitement in the women's drab lives. When the kerosene lamps were lit for the first time on the banks of the Omaka, Jean and Mary and many others walked out in the evening with their families. The streets might not be much brighter, but the women felt a real town came a little nearer with these glimmers in the darkness. Two newspapers they had, now; and at the river wharves several small steamers discharged goods and passengers direct from Wellington.

While Irwin was employed building, life was a little happier for Mary. Her brood of five — the twins' cradles were again filled, this time by George and Brenda — kept her busier than ever. Tom had persuaded Irwin to join the Volunteer Rifles; that provided him with another interest. The days on Molesworth had proved he was a good shot.

Jean, her family no longer round her feet, would attend the ball at Shaws' Hotel in Renwick Town the night of the Volunteers' Match at Hawkesbury. Mary cheerfully made her frock for the occasion; she herself sat at home, although old Annie had offered to mind the babies. She could be trusted to arrive sober, and leave her Square Gin at home; and she was a little — only a little — less slatternly.

Though Mary had said nothing to her husband or her friend, she suspected that this next baby coming rather late in life might arrive unexpectedly early. And it was so. When the three friends reached the cottage in the dawn after dancing all night, they heard a squawking infant.

'Why didn't you tell me you were having labour pains?' Jean demanded. 'Who helped you?'

Then she saw Annie.

'I've delivered dozens,' the successful midwife declared truculently, 'and never a still birth or a lost mother, unlike some of these smart doctors. You're here now. You take off that finery and look after Mistress Mary and the Babe. A strong healthy one that is, for all she's ahead of time.' She dropped her voice to whisper to Jean, 'I wouldn't say the same of the mother, a hard time she's had and not everything as it should be yet.'

Irwin's thanks the old crone brushed aside. 'I'm off to me gin and me bed, it's years since I've not had a drop all night. And if that baby squawks too much, you dip your finger in the gin bottle and let her have a suck.'

Irwin, more rigid in outlook than Tom, was

taken aback. A beer, yes, or once in a while on a special occasion a whisky; but gin or other spirits in the house? Never.

Jean shooed the men off to her home, while she set about putting the kitchen and bedroom to rights, bundling up the soiled linen to wash it in comfort. Not only did she have running water, hot water, but a copper as well, standing out in the yard, to save putting a chimney through the roof. You had to avoid the children's bedroom in the attic, anyway, they'd burn their little hands on the hot tin, Tom said.

He had promised her a lean-to wash-house some day. He was a good man, her Tom. Irwin was more thrifty, but much less understanding. Sometimes Jean would talk about that to her husband. They agreed they could do nothing to lighten Mary's burden, all those steps and stairs of children; Jean and Tom had four of a family, but so spaced that the older ones could take care of the youngest. Jean wondered how Mary could keep count of their ages, all so close and only Jamie really settled at school. Thank the Lord it was not twins again this time.

Rarely had Irwin seen his wife so upset as when he suggested this little one should be christened Jeanie.

'Jeanie still has a place in my heart even if

you've forgotten her,' she sobbed. 'This hateful place has taken her body, but no-one will take the memory.'

For once Irwin did not walk out of the house, as he usually did when Mary's flying temper got the better of her. He had no idea how to handle these outbursts, nor what was the cause of them. Dimly he realised that she was a good wife; this time he tried to console her. She met him halfway and they compromised on Jane for the baby's name. He even began to think about Mary's now voiced dislike of a place where over and over they were rescued by boat, the water levels rose so rapidly.

Floods receded from Maxwell Road, to be followed almost as soon as the cottages were cleared of silt by a violent January storm. The ensuing flood shifted the Omaka Bridge at the west end of High Street; it was five inches off true when the water subsided. And, of course, the allotment at Renwick Town was again under water; and again Irwin's halfhearted attempts at vegetable growing were washed downstream.

In a rare moment, Irwin confided in Tom, discussing Mary's increasing disgust of Blenheim. He wondered if they should move; perhaps Tom could suggest where they could go.

Tom was optimistic. 'Look,' he said, 'they've started the railway line from Picton. Things are looking up, the first cab's clopping along the streets, and there's the theatre. There's the ladies' drapery shop. Buy Mary a dress to cheer her up.'

'Go into a shop for ladies?' Irwin was aghast.

'Well, give Mary the money. Ask Jean to do the shopping,' said Tom impatiently. 'Come on, we'll go down to the pub first, and wet the baby's head, or celebrate being closer to London.'

'12,000 miles.' exclaimed Irwin, ever a slow thinker. 'Oh, you mean those steamers on the Home run. Yes, Mary told me they made the voyage in six weeks or so. We took twice as long.'

'No, the telegraph. Didn't you hear about it? Three hours, then minutes for a message from London.'

'I did hear the staff were coming in from Whites Bay,' Irwin added. 'Suppose they'll be in the Government Buildings. Will that make the message quicker or slower?'

Tom could not answer that question.

But Irwin went on thinking about it. Three hours something for a message, six weeks by steamer. Suppose, he wondered, there were more Cornish folk in the town, would that help? Mary didn't seem to make many friends. Jean was the only one who called often at the cob cottage, and old Annie of whom no gentleman would have approved. Where was that merry laughing girl who had joined so whole-heartedly in the washday picnic up the Taylor River?

He did not think of the demands on body and mind of seven babies in eight years or so. The appearance of twins puzzled him; he had not known of any twins on his side of the family. But he had been so young when his parents died. Perhaps there were relatives somewhere on the Helford?

When he had first asked Mary if she wanted to shift, if he could find the money, she had been interested. But when he went on to suggest going north, she was determinedly against it. There were Maori Wars up there; tales of horror filtered through, sometimes exaggerated, sometimes unvarnished in their cruelty. If a missionary, the Rev. Carl Volkner, could be massacred, no-one was safe. It would have been useless to point out to her that the alleged perpetrator, Kereopa, had been executed, or that Te Kooti was living peacefully in the Maori King's territory. Nor did she realise how many miles separated the Waikato and Taranaki districts from Wellington.

She would not go north. Irwin at this time was equally inflexible about going south. To him that was the Clarence River in flood, snow on the ranges, and gentlemen and servants further south in Canterbury. Let them stay in Blenheim where class barriers had not been erected. Both remembered how Ken had been a friend, although he was the station manager.

At least Irwin and Mary were talking out their thoughts; that was a change from the morose big brown bear. Jean and Tom had persuaded him to take his wife out occasionally, whist drives and the like at Ewart's Hall, rarely the dancing which Mary had so enjoyed; it was whispered that dancing classes might begin at Renwick Town.

While Irwin sometimes wondered about kinsfolk in Cornwall, he did nothing. He had talked to Tom about nominating someone from the Duchy, when the adult would have been required to pay only 20 shillings, — a sovereign, for bedding, blankets and mess utensils for the entire voyage to New Zealand. Since he was slow to take action on a decision of this sort, Irwin did nothing.

With a carpenter's job on the Immigration Barracks, he thought even more about kinsfolk, friends from Cornwall for Mary. Now in semi-permanent real work, he was showing some of the concern of the young man who had rescued her from those louts so many years ago.

Then he and Tom, who was a carpenter's labourer on the same building, would walk home after work, chatting about the town: the soapy water that 'Professor Augustus' drained into Wynen Street from his public baths, the footpath in Auckland Street — they argued about that, Tom saying it was needed, Irwin wondering whether the residents were in the right. They said it would be detrimental to their properties. Both men had a quiet laugh over the latest by-law, forbidding men and boys to stand on the footpath and make insulting remarks to passers-by. They agreed that such behaviour towards women should be stopped. How that could be done they were not quite sure.

The 3000 population of the gold rush days had dwindled by two-thirds. There was plenty of work, and a woollen mill suggested, with a meeting in Aaron Penney's Royal Hotel to consider its establishment.

Now in an upsurge from the era with too few jobs, Blenheim had too few workers. So the Town Clerk, still James Tucker Robinson, set off for Dunedin at the request of the central government. The townsfolk were not too sure about the quality of those

181

immigrants in the south. A report had filtered through, 'by private communication from Otago' that the energies of the police were taxed to the utmost to look after the immigrants who had returned from Invercargill to Dunedin. The gaol and the lockup were over-full, and the Provincial Government was considering sending about 80 of these Asiatics back to England and Ireland. 'Most of the feminine undesirables were ex-inmates of Cork Reformatory', the private communication concluded.

Was the town wise to welcome immigrants? Well, after all, the Town Clerk could make a reasonable selection, for immigrant ships were dropping anchor almost every day in Otago Harbour.

But the officer travelled no further south than Lyttelton. By the time Mr Robinson reached that port, the Agent in Dunedin had advised the Marlborough Provincial Government that 84 people had already been despatched via the *Phoebe* for Marlborough, 'a young and good-looking lot' the advice noted. Included were married couples, 37 single men and three single women. Reaching Wellington on July 24, they were transferred to the *Napier*, which was chartered to transport them to the Wairau Bar, where they would be brought in by lighters to the upriver steamers a day later.

But it was another five days before Mary, with her children joined the community to cheer the first wagon-load of immigrants as they at last reached Wynen St. That warm welcome was needed. They had gone aboard the *Napier* in Wellington only to be buffeted about Cook Strait for five or six hours, tossed about in the rip-tide as the Trelissicks had been, until the Captain found himself less than seven miles off-shore.

The *Napier* returned to Port Nicholson. Those that could be accommodated on the *Phoebe* were set back on board again, and sailed into Picton a day or two later. Others were housed in the Immigration Barracks in Wellington, and ultimately, after crossing the Strait, reached Blenheim in a second wagon.

'Well-assorted and intelligent, likely to make good colonists', they were all made very welcome. Within days those not already engaged were absorbed into the work force and life of the town, four carpenters, a tinsmith, a millwright, an enginefitter and labourers. The following month the *Falcon* brought another group from overseas.

As much to smooth the path of the recently arrived women as to make new friends, Mary and Jean found time for these mainly Cornish folk. They settled in quickly to the cottages, making neat little gardens. Two of the single women found work as cooks in hotels; the third joined the staff at Langley Dale, where she had a friend who had immigrated earlier via Nelson.

Twice a year Polly and Ray would ride down the Awatere to Blenheim, before the snows, and again in the early summer. Though dreams of a coach road or even a good bullock track were far from realised, Atkinson drove his merino sheep from Molesworth down to his Blind River station for shearing. Some improvements had been made, said Ray, especially below Upcot. Downstream from Jordan, the track left the banks of the Awatere, crossing a dozen tiny tributaries, to join the Taylor Pass bullock track into Blenheim.

The newly arrived Cornishwomen, meeting Polly at Mary's home and hearing of her experiences, looked aghast. They themselves were better housed in a bigger town than in their village across the seas. How did this bright woman survive the isolation of the back country and all its demands? they asked. Yet Polly was so contented that Mary wondered if, after all, station life was a better way of living.

From time to time Ken would arrive, unheralded. After Canvastown he had tried his luck in the Central Otago diggings, though the rush was over. He had fetched up in Auckland, which seemed as far away as Falmouth to Irwin. Ken was always prosperous in a quiet way, but restless ever since the days at Molesworth. Perhaps it was the idea of stocking unsuitable country with sheep, trying to produce a decent return for a lessee who would not listen, that had driven him away from a life he had enjoyed.

With no room now in the crowded cottage even for old and well-loved friends, Ray and Polly stayed at the Marlborough. There they met Ken, all three surprised that they had arrived at the same time without any prior arrangement more than ten years since Molesworth days. The party that night was one which Irwin enjoyed, all friends, none merely acquaintances. He was at his most abrupt with people he did not know. Never one to suffer fools gladly, he would retreat from any chatterbox into that morose 'brown bear', as Mary described him.

But here was Ken, his first friend, and Ray, and Tom Jones; and Edward Pascoe, a recent arrival from Cornwall.

Jean and Mary were also amongst close friends, the men whom they knew and their wives, Polly, and Hannah Pascoe, and her sister-in-law Sarah, one of the three single women who had landed a year or two earlier. It was Sarah's adventurous spirit that had encouraged her to follow her brother to New Zealand. Married couples, except for Ken — and Sarah. Once or twice Mary had tried her hand at gentle match-making, only to be warned off with a wicked grin, Ken telling her it was hopeless.

'Once bitten, twice shy,' he would say after she had introduced some delightful young woman. He spoke more seriously this evening. To Mary he confessed that his sons had been adopted by his former wife's second husband; she was never quite clear as to how that divorce had come about in the rigid code of Victorian England. The young men had been educated at the best of public schools, then had undertaken university degrees and professions. They wanted no part of the foreign father, if ever they recalled their very young days on Molesworth. Ken had come to terms with having no family; yet he was tired of living in a valise, as he put it.

When Ray and Polly rode back to Langridge, Ken went with them. He joked about his heart being buried in the Awatere; Jean, always outspoken, told him it was high time he dug it up again.

Mary, noticing good-looking Sarah's blush, thought her friend might be right.

After a week or two up-country, Ken was back in Blenheim, wrinkling his nose at the smell of those pig-sties. 'How do you stand this stench?' he asked Irwin. 'Molesworth air was so clean and fresh.'

'Council's trying to do something about it, trouble is most of the councillors keep pigs themselves.'

'As long as we don't get another flood,' Mary said.

'But that's all fixed, isn't it?'

'I'm not sure, Ken. Heavy rain and thawing snow could do a lot of damage if they came together,' said Irwin.

Jean and Tom joined the friends. 'School holiday tomorrow afternoon,' Jean said. 'You bring your children, Mary, and we'll go across the bridge to watch the first train from Picton.'

'I didn't see the station,' Ken said.

Irwin laughed. 'You can't see what isn't there, Ken, we haven't got one, there's a set of points in that paddock across the river. It's taken three-and-a-half years to get that far, not 18 miles, you guess how long it will take to get the rest of the way into town. There's a bridge to build first.'

'Never mind,' said Tom, 'now we can get to Picton without the bullocky to help us, and it'll take us less than an hour instead of all

187

day with the best of teams.'

'What about asking Sarah to come with us, Jean?' Mary suggested.

'I've asked her, she's baking now for the picnic. We'll all go for a day's fun, we work hard enough.'

Excitement ran high as the bogey wheels rattled across the Plain, the whistle shrieking so constantly that the fireman grumbled that he would run out of steam, and coal, too, he complained. He'd only enough for the return journey, and he wasn't going to look for firewood; not that there'd be any beside the line. The plate-layers had cleared the vicinity, used the debris to boil their billies.

With the railway came a respite, a brief return to the bright outlook of earlier years, a warm enjoyment of all the local events. Only the men sensed this as a lull in anxieties; the women rejoiced in the moments of no floods, no epidemics, no damaging fires. The children were older, less of a tie; household chores completed, Mary, Jean and Hannah, like most of the townsfolk, cheered opposing teams in any sport, no matter who won. Every game was a picnic for the onlookers. Shops were often closed for the day; when the Blenheim Carters and Cabmen took the field against the Blenheim Butchers, Bakers and Blacksmiths the women had to remember their needs the day before. Not a cab was on the rank; if the joint of meat or a loaf of bread had been forgotten, the household went without. No carter for a bag of wheat even if the fowls went off the lay; the horseman from out of town could not get his horse shod when it had cast a shoe. The standard of cricket would not have done for Lords, but what a day it was! The Carters and Cabmen hoped the blacksmiths would not last long at the crease; those mighty shoulders could account for boundaries and sixes without limit, causing often some consternation among the summery parasols and picnic baskets well clear of the field.

14

In the Government Buildings a week later a clerk lifted his head from the desk. 'Smoke?'

Beside him his friend grunted. 'Now I'll have to tot up again. You interrupted.'

The first speaker sniffed, the smell was more pronounced. Was it the lingering whiff of a pipe that needed cleaning? He tried to settle again to the columns of figures. Other members of staff were fidgeting. The supervisor came through from his office, sniffed the air.

'Hot pipe dottle in a waste-paper basket,' he said sternly. 'Who's just knocked out a pipe?'

The younger men stared at him, dumbfounded. They would not dare to light a pipe during office hours. He strode over to each basket in turn, sniffing vigorously. Nothing.

Smoke curled from the far corner, the exterior wall.

'Fire!'

Senior staff were with the juniors in a concerted rush. Someone alerted the Fire Brigade: Jamie, a young telegraph messenger

190

after school and during holidays, about to deliver a government telegram, had noticed the smoke and rushed to raise the alarm. The fire bell over the station clamoured from the tower to volunteer brigadesmen, calling them from work. The blacksmith left his forge to harness the team of matched blacks in the stables.

In the township owners and customers alike were trying to contain the fire with a bucket brigade. It was not the first time they had set this up; the brigade would arrive soon, but while the horses were being harnessed every bucket of water from the tanks at the rear of the building would help. If the tanks ran dry . . . but this was no time to think of the previous weeks without rain, in the smoke and now the flames licking up the wooden walls. Others rescued goods from the nearby shops as fast as they could, willing helpers who had appeared from nowhere colliding with one another in the narrow doorways.

No-one thought at that moment of the records held where the fire had started. Now, as they heard the welcome sound of galloping horses, it was too late.

Heat drove the bucket-brigade back, with blackened faces and choking coughs. The teamster pulled his great draught-horses to a

191

stop, the harness jangling and the brigades-men at a run, linking the hose to the steamdriven pump attached to the tanks carried on the wagon.

'Do what you can, men.' shouted the senior officer. 'Let that building go, stop the fire from spreading.'

They knew, without being told. Thank goodness for the new fire engines. How many times had they turned out to fight hopelessly with the old ones?

Sparks caught in the shingled roofs across the narrow street before they could get enough pressure to that height.

The teamster drove his horses further towards the river, hoping the brigade could stop the flames spreading but realising that his team could be trapped in cross draughts.

Suddenly a shout went up. 'Mind the horses. Right beside them,' Flames burst from beneath a roof, some distance from the collapsing buildings where the fire had first been seen. Another roof caught alight, and a slight breeze sprang up.

It was all the teamster could do to drive his horses clear, well-trained though they were for a situation which animals normally find cause for panic. One after another unrelated fires burst out so fiercely that deliberate kindling must have been the cause. As they damped down one building, a back-draught hurled sparks onto yet another thatched roof. Behind the shops, brigadesmen were trying to soak the raupo clad shacks, for here was the gravest danger.

Tom and Irwin were rushing to warn anyone unaware of the spread of the blaze; just in time in some cases, where the mothers had been sure the fire would be confined to the business area, as it had been in earlier cases. Children screamed as they saw the flames sweeping towards them, their mothers, as they tried to rescue their belongings, too busy to pacify the frightened youngsters. Often Irwin would thrust parents aside as they made one more dash into the home before the thatch went up in flames. The dried raupo flared in one whoosh of total destruction.

The brigadesmen were near the river now, with plenty of water to stop the inferno from spreading; but within the loop of the Taylor and the Opawa 43 shops, offices and homes were beyond rescue. The breeze had dropped, too late to save the tinder-dry shingles and thatching. Even a cob cottage collapsed in the heat as the clay, brittle in the summer dry, crumbled, its thatched roof flaming above the walls. Squealing pigs added to the din and crackle of falling timbers; a pall of black smoke hung over the business area, while beaters with wet sacks tried to confine the fire to its centre; Irwin and his mates chopped away at any building close to the danger zone.

On the river bank, the townspeople watched in dismay and horror. Women whose homes were beyond the reach of any damage made their way round to offer shelter to those made homeless, many with no more than the clothes they were wearing.

The brigade was still pumping water to outlying sites, and the bucket brigade was on the job, working from the outer rim towards the centre where the remains were too hot to approach. It had happened so quickly — one hour, two hours — a sunny, peaceful morning, everybody but one person going quietly about legal business, and now this: no businesses, no goods, worse still no homes for some. At least no lives had been lost.

Police and councillors settled down to talk over the disaster, offering a reward for information leading to the arrest and conviction of the arsonist they were certain was the cause. The menfolk were so furious that the constable feared he would have a lynching on his hands if the culprit was caught.

Scandal pointed a finger at everyone except

a close friend. Later, when the homeless were housed, clothed and fed, Jean, talking to Mary, made a suggestion which was being whispered in the town.

'Those low fellows who climbed onto the hotel roof that night, when the Brigade had the new fire engines, d'you think they had a grudge? D'you think they could have started the fire, Mary?'

'We mustn't repeat that,' she said. 'Besides, they only made a disgraceful noise, you remember?'

'I wouldn't mind the reward,' Jamie tall for his age, his father's build, interrupted. 'A hundred gold sovereigns; gee!'

'And I'd remind you, son, that the reward is only for information leading to the conviction of those responsible,' Irwin advised.

'Do you think someone wanted to claim insurance?' Ken wondered.

'Or wanted to get rid of legal papers,' added Tom. 'Records, valuations, minutes of meetings all gone up in smoke.'

'Old Thomas was mad enough about that fine of two pounds for 'driving his horse furiously in the borough'. He said it bolted on him, but I never knew a man to use a whip when his horse was in the middle of bolting.'

'Surely he wouldn't start a fire just for that' Edward Pascoe objected. 'He's not a bad sort.'

'Perhaps no-one intended such destruction,' said Ken.

'You'll all be so busy with building.' Mary smiled. 'Let's not talk about the fire. Ken, you were going to tell us about your plans before all this happened.'

'Well, that homestead where Murphy lived is empty, Atkinson tells me. He'd rather live at Burtergill, his own place. He might sell the Molesworth lease later, but it's got a couple of years to run.'

'Were you thinking of going back there?'

'If I can have the company I want,' he replied, in a joking manner. 'How about it, Mary? Irwin?'

'With six children?' Mary was shocked into answering before her husband could make up his mind. 'Jamie'd be up the mountains, George in the Acheron and young Brenda with him. No, Ken, no, not for me. Irwin, d'you want to join Ken?'

'They'll be starting new government buildings,' he answered. 'No thanks, Ken, I'll stay here with work I really know how to do.'

'What about that gold they found when they sank the new bore for artesian water supply . . . behind the Royal, Ken?' Edward said. 'You're a prospector, aren't you? Wouldn't that have more promise than a year or two back in the hills?'

'I'm not really a prospector, Edward, more a fossicker. Besides, they were 70 feet down before they found colours of gold. Some of it weighed in at 5 grains, but I doubt if there's anything worth the effort and the initial outlay, machinery and so on.'

'And when Atkinson decides to sell, will you buy the leasehold?' asked Tom.

'No, that's young man's country, Tom, unless you're prepared to set up a whole township for goods and services, so that you're all totally dependent within the station. Anyway, I hear Fuhrmann and Wills are after it. They're sounding out Stedman of St Helens to manage it for them.'

'Ray said you'd been disappointed with the look of the run,' Irwin said. 'What's gone wrong up there?'

'Blasted rabbits — beg your pardon, ladies — the whole hillside moves with the beggars,' he replied. 'But I don't think it's sheep country, I've said that before. They should have stuck to cattle, there's no grazing on the steep slopes even for sheep.'

'So you'll move on again in a year or two, Ken?' asked Mary, rather sadly. When Ken was about, and Tom also, her husband seemed more content with existence. His 'brown bear moods', as she called them, were shorter and less frequent. Once again she wondered if a really black mood, a savage outburst of temper, would clear the fog of misunderstanding that surrounded the family.

'No, I've got a surprise for you. Two surprises in fact, Mary. I hope you'll all like both. I, er — we've decided to settle in Blenheim. I've bought a quarter acre in section 42. Good buying at ten pounds, I thought.'

'My word it was,' Tom agreed. 'That's higher ground there. We'll call to spend a few days if there's another flood.'

Mary's quick ears had picked up Ken's hesitancy, the change from 'I' to 'we'. 'Ken, you said 'we'?'

'I'm taking a cook up to Molesworth for a year or so, Mary.'

Tom guffawed. 'Ken, you weren't the chap who advertised for a wife, were you? No objection to a widow provided she had no more than ten children.'

'No, no, of course not. I didn't advertise for a wife. Or a widow.' He glanced at his friends. For once he had fallen into the trap he set for others, taking Tom's question as if it was intended seriously. 'You took me in that time,

Tom. But my future wife's coming to join us now.'

Jean's comment may have opened Ken's eyes; Mary had not misinterpreted Sarah's blush.

15

Although the wedding was to be quiet, with only the bride's and groom's closest friends at the breakfast, Mary and Jean enjoyed the change in routine. They baked and prepared more food than ever; but it was a change and a challenge to bake for an occasion. Both were busy with sewing, for themselves and the bride.

Tom joked to his friends about being unwelcome at meal-time, teasing Ken about 'More done for you and your wife than there is for me and the family these days. I suppose Mary is neglecting you, too, Irwin?'

'No, meals are always on time. Mary doesn't allow entertainments to interrupt routine.' Tom looked across the bar at Ken. Irwin was heading for one of those difficult morose moods again. Had he wished to go upcountry with Ken? Now that Sarah would be with him, he would need neither Mary as cook-housekeeper nor Irwin as companion-station hand. The trail to the shadow of Tapuaenuku was closed to the Trelissicks; cause, perhaps, for Irwin's regret, but Mary would rejoice.

Soon after the wedding, Sarah and Ken set off for the Taylor Pass, once the snow had melted and the Awatere was fordable again. First to Langridge for a few days with Ray and Polly, then on to Molesworth Homestead, extended by Atkinson to be much more convenient than Mary's early home there.

Sheep instead of cattle did not please Ken. He had not thought much of Bill and Joe; they could be as stupid as sheep, rather certain of themselves and poorly mannered — Joe slurping his tea from his saucer and Bill often using his fingers more than his fork. Poor Mary — thank goodness Sarah would not have to share the meal table with those two.

They might call themselves shepherds, but they could not control their packs of mongrel dogs. They were just as likely to chase off after rabbits as to respond to their owners' whistles and curses. At least the head shepherd was an experienced musterer.

The rabbit warrens which Ken had foreseen were a danger to riders; his favourite Cherry had broken a fetlock and had to be put down. The horses the young men brought to the station were poorly broken in; the saddles were cracked and dry for want of dressing, yet tins of dubbin were kept in store; reins were knotted and frail.

Scab, a disease which Ken suspected could have been passed on by flocks driven overland, from badly affected areas in Nelson, to Canterbury, was an ever-present threat. He had bought tobacco, cut by the chaff-cutter, to boil in water and use the concoction as a dip. He missed Irwin's carpentry skills when the dipping-pen and bath were built. Tanks for lime and sulphur mixes were sledged over Jacks Pass from Hanmer.

When the bullock drawn sledge was late in arriving, Ken rode over Wards Pass to find the reason. Old Bob's language could be heard long before the team could be seen. The sledge was stuck in the creek, and the lead offside bullock would not budge.

Ken suggested that Bob moderate his language and put his trust in Providence.

The bullocky snarled: 'Providence be damned, boss. He's the worst bloody bullock in the whole team, and he's sulked the whole blasted way.'

But the boss reckoned he'd rather drive bullocks than muster those hill country merinos; off the tops for the winter, late lambing, so they could not be mustered from bare pasture as early as cattle, always Ken's choice; all the bothers of lambing with fairly high losses as the ewes were not in good condition; docking, ear-marking.

IRIS NOLAN

◆

SHADOW OF THE MOUNTAIN

Complete and Unabridged

ULVERSCROFT
Leicester

First published in New Zealand in 1992

First Large Print Edition
published 2001

British Library CIP Data

Nolan, Iris
  Shadow of the mountain.—Large print ed.—
  Ulverscroft large print series: general fiction
  1. Large type books
  I. Title
  823.9'14 [F]

  ISBN 0–7089–4423–X

Published by
F. A. Thorpe (Publishing)
Anstey, Leicestershire
Set by Words & Graphics Ltd.
Anstey, Leicestershire
Printed and bound in Great Britain by
T. J. International Ltd., Padstow, Cornwall

This book is printed on acid-free paper

To my late husband Maurie, especially for his dedicated work on the sketch map, and to Rhys, Sharon and Lynne, for their unfailing support in my incursions into Beavertown and the remote valley of the Awatere.

Notes

While landscapes and events are close to fact, the characters have no life beyond the pages of fiction.

Tapuaenuku was the accepted form for over a century, replacing the original **Tapuae-o-uenuku** (footsteps of the rainbow god) gazetted by the N.Z. Geographic Board in 1988.

Acknowledgements

For their willing assistance in research, grateful thanks to the members of the staff of the *Marlborough Express*, and to Mr Rogerson of the Lands & Survey Department, Captain Tom Eckford, and Messrs Alexander Beverley (formerly Town Clerk of Blenheim), Neville Matthews (Past President of the Marlborough Historical Society) and the late L.G. Smith. Gratitude is also expressed to Caltex Oil for permission to use the map outline, and to Sue Gemmell for preparing the sketch for publication.

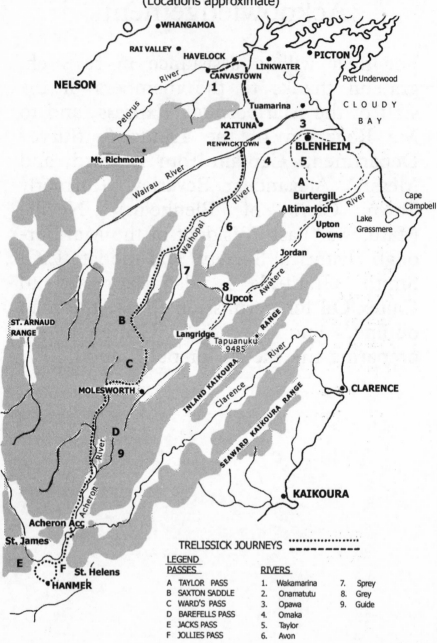

SKETCH MAP
(Locations approximate)

WHANGAMOA

RAI VALLEY

HAVELOCK

PICTON

LINKWATER

CANVASTOWN

1

Port Underwood

NELSON

Pelorus River

Tuamarina

C L O U D Y

B A Y

KAITUNA

2

3

RENWICKTOWN

BLENHEIM

Mt. Richmond

4

5

Wairau River

A

Burtergill

Altimarloch

River

Cape Campbell

Waihopai River

6

Upton Downs

Lake Grassmere

Jordan

7

Awatere River

8

Upcot

ST. ARNAUD RANGE

B

Langridge

Tapuanuku 9485

INLAND KAIKOURA RANGE

C

River

CLARENCE

MOLESWORTH

Clarence River

D

9

Acheron River

SEAWARD KAIKOURA RANGE

KAIKOURA

Acheron Acc

St. James

E

F St. Helens

HANMER

TRELISSICK JOURNEYS · · · · · · · · · ·
– – – – – – – –

LEGEND

PASSES

A   TAYLOR   PASS
B   SAXTON SADDLE
C   WARD'S PASS
D   BAREFELLS PASS
E   JACKS PASS
F   JOLLIES PASS

RIVERS

1. Wakamarina
2. Onamatutu
3. Opawa
4. Omaka
5. Taylor
6. Avon
7. Sprey
8. Grey
9. Guide

To crown all, a pile of carcasses in one corner over a slight slope, and two dogs with the smell of fresh blood on them. Ken shot them on sight. 'If you men can't control your bloody dogs, I'll shoot the whole pack,' he said, when one of the younger men tried to argue that it might not have been his dog that worried the lambs.

'And those two might have taught my good dogs to worry by now,' Ken retorted. 'Let alone how many more of your mongrel curs have the habit.'

Driving the flock to summer country up in the hills was an extra chore this year, owing to shortage of feed; they would have to be brought down again for shearing, much later than in warm areas near the coast. With no woolshed at Molesworth, it was a long drive down the Awatere to Burtergill, Atkinson's own shearing-shed, as Ken had mentioned to Irwin.

They shore any stragglers at Molesworth; so many nicks and cuts did the young men make that Ken picked up the shears himself. He might not be a gun shearer, but he could do a clean, neat job without calling for tar all the time. Then the wool had to be packed down to Burtergill for pressing.

Ken decided he would dip early, as soon almost as the flock came back up the

Awatere; that would save one muster. He was anxious about the future condition of the mob he would turn out beyond Barefell Pass; rumours of scab in St Helen's sheep had reached him. Certainly affected sheep were, by law, to be kept half a mile from boundary fences and from public roads. Was the bullock-track down the Acheron a public road? No-one could answer that query.

And how could a squatter obey that law if, as usual, winter snows had flattened more than boundary fences?

Burtergill kept the Molesworth merinos round the woolshed for a day or two, trying to provide feed before the three-day drive to the Upper Awatere.

Ken, with the shepherds, set off with the big flock in clear weather — no clouds sat on Tapuaenuku. By noon, in the valley heat, the sheep were lagging. Nowhere here to bed them down; it would be cooler in the afternoon, and they could be driven further up river, beyond the gorge.

No warning signs.

Suddenly bitterly cold rain swept into the faces of the shorn animals. The leaders stopped; neither dogs nor humans could move them on. The others, driven on by the shepherds' barking dogs, huddled into the mob, crushing into the slight dip in the track from which the leaders had barely emerged. A smother. The worst experience for a sheep man. Those that did not perish from the sudden cold were suffocated by tail-enders driven over them.

The storm swept on, leaving with as little warning as it had begun. Ken had less than three-quarters of the flock, the rest a pile of bodies stretching along the bullock-track for a quarter of a mile. Others had broken from the mob, rushing pell-mell down a steep rocky bank into the Awatere.

Sam, the owner of the roughest dogs, had the cheek to say it wouldn't take long to dip what was left.

Ken held on to his temper and his fists, contenting himself with dismissing the wretch on the spot, minus notice and reference. 'If I wrote what I thought of you,' he told the self-styled shepherd, 'you'd never get another job, and the words would raise blisters on the paper.'

Any efforts to improve the pasture quality of the home paddocks had to be forgotten while the sheep grazed there, to fit them for the drive into the high country.

The contraption for dipping was ingenious, Ken had to admit, when it worked properly. A three-sided platform tilted towards the dipping pool by means of a counterpoise.

When the sheep tipped against the hinged side above the bath, it swung outwards from the top: ten merinos in the dip. That was simple; but he needed to think up another idea to get the sheep onto the platform. At the end of the race beside it, he put together a railed enclosure — Irwin's help would have been invaluable — which held one sheep; that usually encouraged the silly brutes to walk the plank. He hated sheep; — pushing their stupid heads down with a long crook, being very careful not to overbalance and join them, their fleeces stinking of lime and sulphur as they bleated round the drying yard. Again he could not leave the task for the two men who were paid for it; even the head shepherd would skimp dipping. Ken had noticed, the first day the sheep were tipped in, that they scrambled out immediately, their top-knots still dry. None of the men cared.

These merinos were sure-footed, but no way could they winter over in the high country. He wished, as he had so often before, almost boring his new wife with his complaints, that he had only cattle to tend: much more self-reliant, more sensible and easier to handle. He had not mentioned scrub bulls and wild beasts to her. She was uncomplaining herself, though life was not easy, and very lonely; but the homestead was comfortable now, with separate quarters for the men who were required to cook for themselves with stores provided by the station. Ken's consolation was the job of driving 500 head of cattle down to Hanmer. After the drove, he decided, they would leave the shadow of Tapuaenuku for good.

The newly married couple were fortunate in having set off for their lonely home earlier than was usually practicable. After the mild winter, rain turned Alfred Street into a quagmire; November floods carried the Opawa Bridge at Grove Road downstream after it had collapsed.

Then suspicions about the arsonist were fuelled by the Council's proceeding against a former mayor for shingling a roof without a permit. Shingles could catch fire and spread it, almost as dangerously as the raupo thatch.

The next silly squabble bred the fear of disease, once rain began. Old Jack petitioned the Council to order his neighbour to remove a water closet said to be up against Jack's back door. Neighbour Bill in his turn petitioned the Council to order Jack to stop throwing rotting oranges and onions and other 'household slops of a disgusting nature' under Bill's home.

As Tom said: 'You can't win. It's like these damn piggeries.' He continued, out of the women's hearing 'Hope to God we don't get a flood and more diphtheria.'

Jean and Mary could chat over the good news: the Government Building completed, more immigrants from Cornwall arriving on the *Edwin Fox*, the Wairau Hospital opened with pomp and ceremony — but only in the old Immigration Barracks, with four patients.

There was a shadier side, also. Ed Pascoe was not altogether happy about having asked relatives to sail to this new land; the women could not venture out at night because the idlers in the streets were so rude and threatening. The larrikinism on New Year's Eve worried them all, as it was destructive and not funny at all. Gates had been carried away, shutters removed from shops, and carts and wagons overturned. Groups of hobblede-hoys lounging on the Omaka bridge hurled stones at dogs. Worst of all for Ed, the shrimps he had so enjoyed, caught in the Omaka, now tasted like mud.

The powers-that-be stated that the increase in criminal activity was due to the presence of strangers. Yet the arsonist was still around: fifteen shopkeepers and professional people lost premises in Market Street in a blaze that would have been horrifying had it not been for the earlier 'Great Fire'. Smaller outbreaks were becoming matter-of-fact, routine happenings.

Jean, strolling on the first stretch of concrete footpath, said, 'Blenheim isn't the same as it was.'

'Who would want it to be?' laughed Mary. Every woman had come out in the sunshine to sample that footpath, to walk in light shoes dry-shod and without muddy heels.

'But those pigs,' she told Irwin later, as she described the pleasures of walking on the footpath. 'The stench is worse than ever.'

'The Town Clerk says there are 28 sties in Blenheim alone,' he said. 'How many there are on the outskirts, hidden by flax and raupo, they've no idea.'

Some of that older 'Wild West' flavour remained. Horses were still broken in in the township, and herds of cattle driven through during the day. The by-law prohibiting that was not observed for long; when could a drover get cattle beasts through? And how could he avoid the streets, straddled across east-west and north-south. It took three years to rescind that particular piece of unthinking legislation but, as the townsfolk agreed, the drovers had taken little notice of it, anyhow.

As soon as Sarah and Ken could leave their high country shadow, he set about building their new home, in timber, which kept Irwin busy and contented.

When craftsmanship was wanted, he was easy to live with, Mary discovered. The cheap, hurried jobs he found so frustrating that his moodiness upset the whole family. Not that he admitted it. Mary wished he would discuss the cause of his ill humour; it was not bad temper, he was not harsh on the children, he just ignored them for as long as his brown bear mood lasted. Mary felt uncomfortable, almost disloyal, when she turned to Jean for a discussion that might help. Her friend encouraged her to chat, reminding her that Irwin's failure to talk about his troubles made the problem so much worse.

In the company of his friends the brown moods were not apparent, for which Mary was grateful. She did often wish that he could bring this cheerful attitude home to his family; she understood that he had to relax somewhere, and better at home than at work. She was very glad, especially for the children's sakes, when the moodiness disappeared for a few weeks.

Yet he was so good to them, the lean-to built as a bunk-room for the growing girls, the attic the province of the boys, where high-spirited Jamie was the acknowledged ring-leader. Mary could not find the words for her feelings. If only Irwin could always act like a friend, especially to Jamie who needed his fathers affection and friendship particularly at his age. If only the father who used to take him fishing could come back again. Disappointment had shadowed that warmth which showed for such a little time.

16

Ken's house completed, he busied himself with often frustrating community affairs. He was one of the first to lobby the Council to buy the gasworks from its private operators, who set a price of £8000.

'The idiots,' Ken exclaimed to Irwin. 'They'll have to buy the undertaking in the end, and it'll cost double the amount quoted.'

One red-letter day in 1880 saw the train steam into Blenheim, another occasion for a picnic holiday when the new railway station was crowded that first day in May. It had taken over three years to cross the river.

But other projects were stalled, as they had been before, by public outcry or by the lack of records. Ken had not been in the district when the Government Buildings were burnt down; he wasted some time blaming inefficiency when he learned that one ratepayer owned a fourteen inch wide strip through the middle of another ratepayer's shop. However, he was most angered by the public outcry over the Council's proposal to raise Maxwell Road one foot.

'More stupid fools live here than anywhere

else,' he grumbled to Irwin. 'Saying that scheme would turn Blenheim into a lake. Well, if those self-centred idiots get flooded out, damned if I'll row a dinghy to their rescue.'

'Perhaps they think we're safe now from big floods,' said Irwin pacifically. 'We haven't had water over the garden for years. And you know it used to rise higher than the window-sills.'

'We haven't had winter snows, solid rain, a sudden thaw and spring tides all together, either,' Ken objected. 'You had a look at the Taylor river-bed lately?'

'No, Ken. Why?'

'We'll go up there one Saturday late afternoon. We might take our rods. Trout'd be a change from hogget.'

Ed Pascoe joined them on their expedition. Each succeeded in landing a meal of brown trout, but it was Irwin who caught a four-pounder. Good-sized fish still rose to the angler's lure or huhu bug, as the case might be.

But the joy of landing fish contrasted with their concern about the river. They walked home very thoughtfully, saying little; Tom and Irwin, who had fished the river for many years, were particularly silent. The bed was filling with shingle, washed down in each successive flood. It would not be long before there would be no margin at all in the town for freshes.

Ken broke the silence. 'Guess the Council doesn't care. The councillors and senior staff all live on higher ground.'

'I heard old Migsworth say the sooner floods washed away the old cottages the better,' commented Tom.

'I know the Council's short of funds, but the owners of the cottages can't afford to leave them,' Ken said. 'No-one's getting much for meat and wool, many of the rates are not paid.'

Ed broke in. 'Too many councillors are farmers, that's the trouble, they won't increase the rates. As you say, Ken, people with money live on higher ground.'

'I'm up there, too, Ed, but that doesn't mean I don't worry about the others liable to be flooded out. It costs more to repair roads and so on than it would to clear the river-bed; they could use the shingle, anyway.'

'We'll put you on the Council, Ken,' Irwin said seriously. 'Someone needs to worry about those cottages, they're mostly well cared for. All the tumbledown raupo huts have been swept away.'

But the next news over-rode concerns about flooding. At first, rumours of Maori discontent in Taranaki whispered round the town. Then the Volunteer Rifles, of which Tom, Ken, Irwin and Jamie were members, was asked by the government to send a contingent to help the constabulary in the area. Those men, expert with the rifle and well-drilled, were happy to volunteer.

Not happy at all were their wives. And Mary had Jamie to think about, as well as Irwin. Tom was looking on the trip as an adventure, Jean said; Ken felt it would all be over before they got there. Having spent some years in the north, he could not see any more full-scale land wars developing. But he would go, of course, added Sarah. There were no children for him to consider. Jean's family was nearly grown-up; but both women agreed that Irwin's place was near his home, not far away in the other island.

He volunteered with the others; the Three Musketeers and Jamie, they called themselves. But they became the Three Musketeers, without Irwin. To his disgust he was rejected on health grounds.

He was furious. 'Nothing wrong with me,' he stormed, 'just as fit as you, and younger, too.'

'Perhaps your time in the mines caused some trouble,' Ken suggested.

'Twenty years ago.'

'Maybe the conditions at Canvastown had

something to do with it.'

'You were there longer than I was,' Irwin grumbled.

'Look, it's hard enough for Mary to see Jamie go. She needs you and so do the children. One of us should stay back. You've seen how easily the Taylor could flood. And we never know when that arsonist might strike again — he's not been caught.'

Irwin grunted. 'I'm caught here by fires and flood. Anyway that scoundrel only destroys business areas.'

'Was the Wesleyan Chapel a business, Irwin?' Ken had rarely found Irwin so cantankerous.

'Nobody lived there.'

'They told me houses went up in flames in that big fire when I was at Molesworth. Was that story a figment of the imagination?'

Irwin had the grace to falter. 'Ee-er-no, but they caught fire by accident, I'd think.'

'You stop and look after Mary and the children, and keep an eye on our households, too, please, Irwin. You'd make any excuse to go with us.'

'And I'd stay up north, too,' Mary's husband muttered under his breath.

The three women waved their menfolk off to the Maori Wars, as the train pulled out of Blenheim station bound for Picton, and the

216

steamer for the north. It was high adventure to Jamie, but his mother recalled stories of the Waikato, wondering if she would ever see her beloved eldest son again. Such a little time, less than two short years, she recalled, blinking away tears, since they had all so cheerfully and noisily greeted that first train into the station. Who would be on the next one they decided to meet? she wondered sadly.

Irwin was no comfort. Even more morose and sullen than in his brown bear mood, he fumed about not being allowed to help his adopted country. Mary would never know that his dreams of escape to the north had been shattered. The day after the train left he walked, silent, out of the cottage. Mary hardly dared ask where he was going.

'To that wilderness at Renwick Town,' he grunted. 'Expect me when you see me.'

He had not bothered with that land since the flood before the last had strewn more boulders over the small cleared patch. For years he had struggled with the heartbreaks: seeds washed out in the kowhai floods, vegetables maturing when January storms destroyed everything. He had given up in the end, realising that what his aunt had left him was worthless.

Why would he go back there, Mary wondered, to upset himself still further?

17

Irwin leaned on his shovel, looking in despair at the devastation. He had left those cackling hens — yes, even Mary could drive him daft with her chatter once she and Jean were working together. He had suggested that Mary go down and help Jean first, ignoring the fact that floodwaters would still have not receded from Tom's place.

God knows, he thought, the women were quiet enough while they watched those grey waters cover the road, and then steadily sneak up to the fence.

Now Mary was whirling through the cottage like a tornado. Everything had to be done at once — now — this morning — yesterday. And the way she scrubbed at that poor quality paint on the paling fence. He had told her to leave it, put up with the tell-tale brown stain, everyone in town had a floodmark somewhere. But no, she couldn't abide that stale, muddy smell, and she couldn't abide the coloured reminder of it either.

She made a man's life a misery when she set about spring-cleaning, with all the curtains down, and pillow covers washed. Those two precious feather-filled ones meant you dare not open a door while she was busy emptying or filling the twill envelopes. That week there was only one thing to do, go out. And Irwin got out.

After a flood, life was even more unbearable. You could lend a hand to all your friends, pick up an odd job; but it was all women's work, cleaning shop-fittings or shelves, or drying out papers for the offices. Until the ground was fit to dig, you couldn't replant your garden. And now his friends were away at the wars.

So, shovel over his shoulder, Irwin had trudged the miles to Renwick Town. Trudged? He had nearly lost a wellington boot in that muddy bank near the crossing; the bridge was still standing, but so rickety he wondered if he would be able to return. One more tree-trunk battering the dam of debris against the piles, and the bridge would collapse.

Every woman living on the lower levels was busy flinging out rag mats and sacks, blankets — on the clothes-line if they had one — fences festooned with what looked like great fat eels drying in the sun down at Tuamarina.

It had not been one of the more damaging floods at Blenheim, despite the men's fears of the Taylor shingle deposit: Some of the protection schemes and drainage ditches were beginning to work. But up here some quirk of the current had tormented Irwin's ten acres.

The vegetables that should have fed his family had gone — that was to be expected. The soil had gone, too, or else the Wairau had dumped all its load of flood-borne boulders on the cleared area. And with them twisted branches, trees — why hadn't he brought an axe with him? — a dead sheep, with the muddy wool already steaming in the sun. On the lower side where flax and gorse had defied his half-hearted efforts, the river had made a beach of sorts. Dead hens, half-buried in silt; there was a rooster who would no more wake its owner at daybreak.

Further in — how could it have been carried as far as that? — a great mound which turned out, on closer inspection, to be a steer swollen almost to bursting, like the poisoned beast on Molesworth. Already the stench was putrid. He could dig a pit to bury the sheep, but a well-grown steer! He hoped the hawks soaring overhead would quickly pick its bones clean. That looked like a dog-kennel; it could be some use. Sickened he found in it a black and white collie dog, strangled by the chain in its frenzied attempts to escape rising waters somewhere upriver.

Irwin hurled his cap on the muddy ground and jumped on it.

'What useless bugger wouldn't let his dog off the chain?' he yelled to the cluttered flax bushes.

He buried the dog. When he tugged at the sheep, the wool came away in his hands. Milk fever had done its worst before the flood carried that carcass down the river. The wool would not be any use, even for Mary's spinning-wheel.

Irwin sat on one of the boulders until the sun neared the peaks of the St Arnaud Range, as far from the dead steer as possible, his back turned to the disaster. Far away to the south, sunset flamed for a moment on the topmost peak, Tapuaenuku.

What had someone said long ago? Footsteps of the rainbow god? Footsteps of doom, Irwin decided.

18

For Mary life had to go on. Three children to send to school, with the other 362 that attended the borough schools. Margaret was behind the counter in the ladies' drapery store, Michael, like his father, in the building trade.

Jean came round, then Sarah — lonely, both of them — and concerned for their husbands. But they were even more concerned for Mary; did she think Irwin was setting off for the wars on his own?

Three more days dragged by with no word.

'Should you ask the police if they have seen Irwin?' Hannah, visiting Mary, asked.

'Oh no! My husband would be very angry,' she replied. 'He'll come back when he feels like it.'

Then the crew on board the *Napier* reported they had seen a man fall overboard from another vessel. They were not sure if he had fallen or jumped, or been pushed. They had manned a dinghy at once, but had not found the body. The *Marlborough Express* recorded that no-one had been reported missing.

Jean and Sarah went at once to Mary, fearing that the only missing man they knew had been drowned.

'Irwin said he was going to Renwick Town,' Mary objected stubbornly, trying to convince herself. 'He couldn't have been on that ship.'

Persuaded at last by her friends, she talked to the newspaper editor. He published a report that a man named Irwin Trelissick 'who had started out for Renwick Town some days earlier' was reported missing.

That brought all the neighbours and friends, even old Annie, really ageing now, to Mary's door. Awkwardly none of them knew quite what to say. Was she now a widow? And what would her husband do, if by any chance he returned?

Annie, who had seen something of Irwin's black moods, was in no doubt. 'You'll see, Mistress Mary, he'll be back. And he won't half be cross with you for telling all Blenheim he'd cleared out.'

'Please, Annie, don't say that. He didn't clear out,' Mary said loyally. 'He went to work on his property at Renwick Town.'

'Well, he's not there now, or that newspaper would have brought him home, surely,' said Sarah. 'I wish Ken wasn't at those Maori Wars, he could have looked for Irwin.'

'Or Jamie, if he'd been here,' Mary added, sadly.

Another day dragged by. Then Jean arrived, all smiles, with the newspaper. She looked so cheerful Mary thought the War might be over. However, it was a letter to which she pointed. Dated at Tuamarina, it read: 'I met a man named Irwin Trelissick on Kaituna Road three days after the reported drowning. He was carrying a swag, and told me he was making for Picton and a steamer.'

That was Irwin, he never wanted to chat to passers-by. It seemed that Jean might have the right idea. He was on his way north, if not to Taranaki.

Then the news came through that the war was over, without a shot being fired. The Constabulary, accompanied by the Volunteers, had marched on Parihaka to arrest the chiefs Te Whiti and Toru, the former chief apparently grateful that difficulties largely caused by tribesmen from another area had been resolved. Both chiefs were released a week later, Toru to his own hapu in the King Country.

Irwin walked into the cottage, saying nothing, as if he had been all the time at Renwick Town. The black mood still had its grip on him. Years later he would admit to Mary that he had been fossicking for gold, first at Onamaluta — that was why he told the passer-by that he was on his way to Picton — and then at the Wakamarina diggings. Too late she would learn that he was dissatisfied with the bare wages paid in the town. But she never did find out if he had heard that he was reported missing.

Before the Volunteers were welcomed home, the arsonist struck again, with many buildings in the central area burnt down.

Industry was growing in the town, but not in the funny-peculiar manner of a reported gunpowder factory run by an Arab. None of Mary's friends could understand why a soap factory should be started; they had no use for bought soap. Their daughters had already learnt to render down mutton fat, put it in the copper, or a kerosene tin with the top cut off, add the right amounts of caustic soda and water, and boil up the mass. That cleaned the copper, too.

Protests were many; settlers wanted the Nelson-West Coast proposition for a main trunk railway line through those districts, scrapped. More than half a century later Blenheim would have its wish granted, and the Main Trunk line would be completed down the East Coast.

Annoying Irwin was the by-law requiring him to replace the shingles on the roof with non-combustible material. His family had lived under shingled or thatched roofs for generations. If 'they' captured the arsonist, there would be no fire danger, he stated loudly. Why didn't 'they' do the job they were paid to do? He was not sure whether he was referring to the police or to the council, or the government.

Jamie was waiting his turn in the store in Market St when shouts sent him to the doorway. Galloping hooves drummed in the street. As he reached the path, the baker's cart shot past him, drawn at a crazy speed by a runaway piebald horse. People standing about scattered to the safety of shops. From the banging doors of the cart, frightening even more the usually placid horse, cascaded loaves of bread.

Jamie was not the only one to cash in on discount bread. Boys appeared from everywhere, like a lolly scramble at a picnic; they picked up every loaf they could see, regardless of mud. More circumspect, Jamie collected only four clean double tin loaves before melting quietly from the scene.

The baker, 'Old Doughy', was jumping up and down with temper, torn between the loss of his baking and the danger his horse and delivery van could cause. He was not too concerned: the piebald would run out of breath sooner or later. He discovered it quietly grazing on a neighbour's unfenced lawn a mile or so down the road.

Carrying on the conversation with Mary about the expense of re-roofing, Irwin turned to his son as Jamie arrived home in high spirits.

'Where are we to get money to buy iron?' he asked of them both.

His son disregarded the question. 'Never mind about iron just now, father, I've brought us all a present.'

He produced four large loaves, to his mother's distress.

'We don't buy bread, Jamie. You know I bake our own.'

'And very good it is, too, mother. But you can have a rest from baking the next batch,' he teased, in his incorrigible way.

Irwin could never understand his tall son's sense of humour. 'You tell me where you got that,' he demanded, the black mood sweeping over him. 'Spending money on bread your mother could bake while I'm worrying about the new by-law.'

Jamie, unlike his mother, was rarely in awe of those moods. 'I wish you had been there to see it,' he laughed. 'Though it wasn't really funny till it was all over and no-one was hurt. 'Old Doughy' left the doors of his bread cart open while he was delivering in Market Street and the piebald bolted. Bread everywhere. And some of it didn't roll in the mud.'

'I suppose everyone in town has baker's bread tonight,' Mary said.

'I'd think so. The children weren't too particular about a bit of mud as well. I must tell Maisie about it,' Jamie said as he went off to visit Jean's daughter.

Anxious to change the subject, Mary suggested there could be a wedding soon, with her the mother of the groom and Tom the father of the bride. Irwin grunted in reply.

He did not grunt when screams of 'Murder! Murder!' awakened them one midnight. He joined the other men alarmed by the shouts in a search for the victim — old Annie, dead drunk and sitting in a swamp yelling at the top of her slurred voice. The armed posse, giving up the hunt for the would-be killer, heaved her out of the bog. They carried her home with difficulty, on the way rousing Jean and Mary to put her to bed.

The hotelier was in a sad way. He had provided coils of rope in the upstairs bedrooms, with fire ever on his mind. In the morning he found three guests had decamped with their bag and baggage, shinning down the rope, leaving unpaid bills behind them.

'Everyone can burn to death for all I care,'

he grumbled to Tom. He was angrier still when Tom pointed out that fire escapes were supposed to be installed.

A plague of rats persisted, causing more alarm when very young children were bitten. Traps were set beside the waterways, but they caught only eels, supplying free breakfasts for many.

And there was Archdeacon Butt, getting round his parish very quickly on the contraption he had bought in England. Mary doubted if it was proper for an Archdeacon to travel on a three-wheeled 'tricycle'. He should have been driven, she thought.

Jamie was intrigued. He peered at it whenever he had the chance, with the intention of making one for himself if he could find wheels.

Some of the lucky women, Sarah and Jean among them, had gas piped to their homes. Sarah was happy about it; Ken had explained clearly, and she had seen gas used for heating or cooking in city areas they had visited together. Jean was not so sure, although Tom was proud of those gas lamps, with the mantle that needed only a turn of the switch and a match.

Irwin in his dour way told Mary that he thought he might find enough money to have such lamps. There was always wood or coal to keep the Orion stove alight. She had progressed in 20 years from the camp oven on the open fire to a cast iron wood-burning range. Some day Irwin might think about a boiler for hot water; meanwhile the heavy oval boilers and large iron saucepans heated all the water Mary wanted. The copper was in the yard, as Jean's had been so long before. When the older children married, Irwin would turn the lean-to into a wash-house, he said; somewhere to put gumboots and his wet oilskin.

Mary was glad not to have gas. Something you could not see providing lighting was uncanny. As for the smell of kerosene lamps, and blackened glass if you turned the wick too high or it needed trimming, you learned to do the right thing. Gas smelled also.

The low prices of the 1880 season had improved, but trying to raise £250 towards the cost of a district hospital demanded all of Ken's persuasive personality. He gathered his friends round him for suggestions; none of them could afford to give money, he knew, but they would knock on doors, talk to people, attend whist drives and lecture evenings, each activity raising a little towards the target. The younger group he left to Jamie and Jean's daughter, Maisie. They could organise a dance in the Ewart Hall.

It was not a large sum, Ken explained to Irwin. There were nearly 500 children now in the local schools: half a sovereign for each, and with the government contribution of double the target (providing the locals could reach it) they would have a real hospital.

Tom objected. 'Ken, you can't look at it that way. Six, say, of those children may be from one family. Their parents are much worse off for cash than you, with no children at school yet.'

Edward Pascoe agreed. Coming to Blenheim in the mid 70's on a nominated passage, he had been in permanent work ever since. He had lost pay when the 21 telegraphists struck, to resist increased hours and overtime, and paid the £2 fine like all the others. But the couple had been housed, like most of the later immigrants, above flood level. Much had been learned about the swamps, drains and rivers in the meantime. Edward had no struggle to survive in Blenheim, though he had experienced his share of hard times in Cornwall.

Ken saw their point. But he had had no intention of assessing family donations on the number of children at school, which was what his friends assumed.

'I see what you were thinking, Ed,' Ken said. 'Thanks. Because if you fellows misunderstood, then the public certainly would. I thought it could be a way of explaining how much we need the hospital for some of those 500 children.'

He battled on with fund-raising, receiving knock-backs sometimes from people who could afford to give generously, and from those on a hand-to-mouth existence donations which could have provided one more much-needed meal.

'It's not the rich and the poor that bother me,' he told Irwin. 'It's the miserly and the generous-hearted I don't forget — the takers and the givers.'

Almost a year later 50 acres of Amersfoot were placed at the disposal of the hospital committee. When the existing facility was publicly described as a wretched, bug-ridden edifice, the committee set to work in earnest to remedy the situation.

Meanwhile Ken soldiered on. The 200 horsemen riding with the Wairau Hunt Club — supposing they each give a donation equal to the cost of a bundle of hay? He was full of ideas. The Blenheim Preserving Company wanted five tons each of peaches, plums, apricots and pears. Prices were not very good, but most of the fruit would be picked by the families from home orchards: could each give a 'few bob' from their sales? As for the

150,000 rabbits the company wanted, there was no shortage. How about trapping or shooting for the new hospital?

Sarah was anxious about her husband's dedicated involvement. 'He drives himself silly about that hospital,' she said to Mary. 'I know he's on the committee and the Council, but he's trying to do everything himself.'

'Tom told Jean and me that no-one else can see the need,' Mary said. 'All they're thinking of just now is replacing Gouland's ferry with a bridge.'

'But they've got all the country districts to contribute to that.'

'Not too many people living in Blenheim bother about using the ferry,' Mary agreed.

Tom was cross about what he called another tax.

'Half a sovereign for a trout fishing licence,' he grumbled to Edward. 'Most of us like a bit of trout for a change, helps out the wages, too. That means ten bob a fish if I catch only one during the season.'

'That'll be the day when you land only one a season,' Edward laughed. 'Besides, you'd have to count four-pounders as more meals than the two-and-a-half pounders Ken and I mostly hook.'

'I'm going to chase up that 24 pounder in

233

the Taylor,' Tom said. 'That'd be value for money.'

'You can't use gelignite or explosives, though,' Tom joked.

Tom missed out on that fish. The conditions of the licence said nothing about using rod or line; the Secretary of the Acclimatisation Society caught the monster with his bare hands. Tom's guess as to its weight fell short; it weighed 24½ pounds.

Jean, when Tom told her about it, commented: 'No wonder the swimming pool seemed to be getting smaller and smaller.' In reality, as they both knew, the river-bed was still filling with shingle.

Jamie was settled, his mother thought, with his marriage to Maisie shortly to take place. Mary was sewing furiously, the bride's gown, Jean's frock, her own as mother of the groom. She had not much time to wonder what George and Michael might be doing with their spare time. It was a pity Irwin wouldn't tackle that ten acres with their help.

With the preserving company wanting fruit, Ken had tried to persuade Irwin to plant fruit trees. Apricots should do well; summer heat to ripen, heavy winter frosts, good drainage in partly clay soil. Irwin rejected the advice. He seemed determined that his only heritage should remain useless.

Although sports groups were active — the Rowing Club pulled from Blenheim to the Wairau Bar in an hour and 20 minutes — the younger ones were not occupied enough to stay out of mischief. Every time some prank was reported, George and Michael would face questions from mother or father or both. Jean's older boy was out of it, but she would cross-examine Jim, younger than Michael, as if they were in a court of law.

Fortunately for the friends, the five boys accused of tin-kettling a newly married couple were recognised and convicted.

Jamie thought that was a bit rough on the boys. 'Scrooge was rather old for a honeymoon with a 20-year-old,' he said, 'that was why the boys did it.'

'What will you and Maisie do if they wake you on your wedding-night?' Margaret asked.

'We won't be silly enough, or so miserable, as to stay in Blenheim that night, Sis. But if there's a tin-kettling to wake us when we come back, I'll shout the lads a beer. Darned if I yell for the peelers. We're getting too prim altogether.'

But he felt the next ploy was too dangerous to be funny. The blacksmith found a pound of gunpowder in his bellows, luckily before he used them.

The same impish inspiration was behind

the next prank; but the upright citizens of Blenheim were unimpressed by the sheer brute strength of the action. Their prized carronade from the whaler *Caroline* had been exchanged for the Wairau Plain by Captain Blenkinsopp, that exchange with Te Rauparaha and other chiefs being indentured on 26 October, 1832, at Kakapo Bay. Later, as all pioneers learned very early, the transaction was denied by the chief, his denial leading to the Wairau incident. Noone was concerned half a century later with the whys and wherefores: did the Maori chief covet the eight pound calibre carronade? Did he misunderstand how much of the area Captain Blenkinsopp expected in return?

Most citizens had forgotten where the carronade was — until they found it rolled down the bank into the Omaka River one frosty morning. Just as well it was not in the Opawa, Jamie commented, in eight feet of water at low tide.

Diphtheria struck again. Sarah's three-year-old was very ill, but pulled through while other children died. Mary, remembering little Jeanie, shared the nursing with Sarah. Doctors were unsurprised by the epidemic; the streets were still filthy, wet and deplorable, according to a reporter on the staff of the *Marlborough Express*, 'more like a primaeval swamp into which one sinks ankle deep after rain'. No wonder disease could take such a hold.

The Mount Tarawera eruption jolted most out of their local preoccupations. The shock felt there, and the fine volcanic dust, which showered even the decks of ships well out in the Tasman, sent some of the less hardy looking for passages 'Home'. They would not live any longer in this land of volcanoes.

Some were so near panic that Ken tried to tell them that the volcanoes, sleeping or extinct, were in the North Island. He was also uncomfortably aware that they were living on a fault line, and earthquakes were never extinct. Even their sleeping pattern, as he explained to Edward, was quite unpredictable.

And what could they do about it? Ken had seen round Wellington coastlines an extra 10 or 12 feet of uplift that made it easier for those who had followed Weld and Clifford, to drive their sheep past the Orongorongo Range to Lake Ferry in the Wairarapa. Irwin remembered the Captain telling them how the beds of the rivers had changed, about the same time, Ken thought probable.

Three months after the eruption, tumbling chimneys reminded them all that they lived on a fault-line. It happened so suddenly there was no time to be afraid,

Mary confessed to Jamie.

The fire and flood which followed could have nothing to do with the earthquake. Or could it? Ken wondered. Perhaps a river-bed had narrowed, as occurred in other districts, or the bed had filled. Certainly it was one of the worst floods for years. Jamie, one of the fire-fighters, was up to his ribs in flood waters while they tried to put out a fire in the wool-store.

Afterwards he raised a reluctant smile from his father, with the comment that they had more than enough water to fight the fire but it was all in the wrong place.

Many families took refuge in the second storey of Parker's Flour Mill. Those who wanted flour would need afterwards to order it from Picton, with all the grain, processed or unprocessed, saturated on the ground floor. The mail did get through from Nelson; once again the rider swam his horse through 14 streams between Havelock and Blenheim.

The housewives and the shopkeepers settled down to clean up once again. Mary was faced only with silted floors; such of the Council's work as had been done had helped to keep the flood levels lower in the neighbourhood of the Trelissick cottage. The Taylor had not been quite such a threat as the friends had expected.

Shop assistants had unwelcome unpaid holidays; it was the owners who cleaned up, replacing stock which had been hurriedly moved upwards in the short warning period. School was closed, the young folk trudging about in gumboots, sometimes helping, mostly just looking. Jane, in her early teens, was working alongside her mother. No longer did Mary bother about scrubbing the fence. Like all the others, she was taking floods for granted, her feelings of disappointment and disgust merged into a numbed acceptance of all-to-common disasters.

The fifteen-year-olds, George and Brenda, wandered off to the riverbanks. Nothing useful would float down and settle beside the bank, that was asking for two impossibilities. But, incurably optimistic, they watched the current. The day was warm and sunny, bliss to be outside, and if they kept well away, father could not find a task for them.

Occasionally stock floated down, caught up in tree roots that swirled in the thickened eddies, sometimes dropping its load as it reared up on an under-water snag. George pointed upstream, his mouth open in amazement.

'What is it, George? Not a body?' Brenda's warm brown eyes were not as long-sighted as George's blue ones; she was ready to run from such horrifying debris. Drownings had been reported.

A sheep, upright as if it was swimming, even walking in water, it was so steady, came slowly down, out of the power of the current.

The twins grabbed one another, with a babble of 'It couldn't be — we're seeing things.'

As the sheep came abreast of them, they knew they were not seeing things; they were gazing at a once only event.

Drowned the sheep might be, though why wasn't the carcass on its side in that case? But very much alive, fur drenched yet erect with fear was a rabbit tucked in the long wool near the neck. And behind it, bedraggled and clinging with frightened claws was a tabby cat.

Brenda rushed to the water's edge. Could she rescue the pets? Before she could take one step too many, George was grabbing her powerfully round her waist.

'No. No. Let them go. You can't get them. Don't be stupid, Brenda.'

Tears came into her eyes as she watched the strange cargo drift out of sight.

Her twin was excited. 'Let's rush home and tell Jane, she'll believe us. I know mother and father won't.'

'Nor will Jamie,' Brenda said, 'but we did

see a cat and a rabbit on a sheep.'

'Nobody will really believe what we saw, Brenda,' said George thoughtfully. 'So we'll tell them we saw a sheep rescue a cat and a rabbit. Pity the cat was bigger, it could have been a pillion passenger.'

'They certainly won't believe the rescue story.'

'We don't know the animals won't be rescued in the end. And if we're not going to be believed anyway, we might as well tell a good story.'

Brenda's tears were forgotten in the excitement as they sloshed home.

Jane's reaction was halfway to belief; then she asked if they truly saw the sheep rescue the animals. Irwin told them to forget the nonsense, and go round to Auntie Jean to be some use. Mary almost ignored the story and the reactions.

It was a gleeful pair who waved a copy of the *Marlborough Express* at the family a few days later. 'It did happen, see. A cat, a rabbit and a sheep.'

Mary sighed, hardly responding. She was always tired, yet she now had so little to do. Jamie married, with a tiny son and daughter; twins certainly ran in the family. Margaret marrying impatiently young, to live with her farmer husband in North

241

Canterbury somewhere near the Clarence, where Ken and Irwin had driven those cattle twenty-five or so years earlier. Irwin not yet fifty, but always seeming ten years older, quiet, withdrawn, impatient with the young people's chatter. They were good children, thought Mary, cross with her dour husband. Never a word of praise from him, yet they all took a share; delivery jobs after school for the younger boys, sewing and minding infants for the girls. Michael had taken himself off to Christchurch with a cadetship in the Post and Telegraph office. Maybe Edward Pascoe's influence had been felt there.

Perhaps Mary would talk to Jean, it must be the change of life they discussed sometimes. Old Annie, with all her midwifery experience, might have helped.

She did not want to think of Annie; slatternly, gin-sodden, but one in a thousand when it came to coaxing reluctant babies into the world. But all those years after she had yelled 'Murder!' from the swamp — did she have a premonition? — some unknown brute from the goldfield had bashed her head in. The police had not found him; he was well away on a ship bound for Sydney when a neighbour wondered why she had not seen Annie for a few days. The beast had ransacked her shack for her tiny hoard without success. Searching for clues, the police found it, with a note scrawled in an ungainly hand, addressed to Mary and Jean: 'Bury me decent, ladies, share out any that's left to all your kids.'

19

Brenda, who intended to be a nurse, since Florence Nightingale decades earlier had made that an acceptable profession, was hoping to enter a training school in one of the New Zealand hospitals. She looked across the room at her mother. More than sorrow about the past momentarily shadowed her drawn face. With a whispered word to George, Brenda slipped out to fetch Jean.

She needed no more than one glance, either. That glance convinced her that another baby would be born in the cob cottage. She sent George for the doctor, fearing complications; bundled the unnoticing Irwin off home to keep Tom company during what might be a long night, and Jane to Jamie and his wife. Brenda could help her; it would not be many months before she would be handling more unpleasant cases in hospital.

Irwin was slightly unbelieving. Mary hadn't said anything, hadn't complained about pains.

'Did she ever?' Jean snapped, at the end of her patience. 'For goodness sake, I'll have

Tom round here soon, asking when I'm coming home. Get out, Irwin. We'll send for you if we need you. I'll send George to stay when he gets back.' She feared Irwin would be needed: to say goodbye to his wife.

Their doctor arrived with a midwife. Like Dr Horne of so long ago, he took notice of his patients even when they had not attended surgery. He was not surprised. Between them they coaxed a reluctant baby into the world and slapped life into it. It was difficult to say which of the parents was more amazed. Family and friends rejoiced over Mary's delight, and Brenda's, who took on the care of the baby while the mother made a very slow recovery.

Indeed, Mary dragged a wing, as she said, all through the troubles of 1887. No sewage disposal implied a constant threat of disease; winter brought a cluster of earthquakes, none of them really damaging, but each advancing a query about a major shock.

At one stage Irwin did brighten up. Land at St Leonards was selling for 22 sovereigns for 50 acre lots; perhaps he could find a buyer for his ten acres. As usual, he had thought about it for too long. Good land, cleared, was available. No-one wanted head-high gorse and toi toi that should have been slashed years earlier.

Little William's chortles brought no smile

to his father's face; the brown bear mood was almost permanent.

Hannah Pascoe was horrified when Jean burst out laughing at the story of the latest rascality. She apologised afterwards, saying she supposed it wasn't funny for the victim, and one should stand by women. But it was a question of who nagged whom the most, and whether dirty old Eliza received more black eyes from that beery lout of a husband than she gave him.

Tom thought it served Eliza right. If he'd a wife like that, he'd not only have beaten her and dunked her in the well three times, he'd have left her there the last time.

'Men,' Hannah sniffed. 'They're never on our side.'

'Well,' said Jean reasonably, 'the Court didn't think it much of a crime; they fined Albert only a sovereign and a half.'

'And what call had Eliza having the law on her husband, I'd like to know,' demanded Hannah, changing her ground. 'They should have kept their fights to themselves.'

'They never do,' Jean said. 'You can hear them all over town. We're two blocks away, and I doubt they ever have a row without letting us know, and every other soul in Blenheim. They're rowdier than ever 'Puffing Billy' was.'

The arsonist struck again. By this time the citizens were considering forming a vigilante group. Certainly Ken, Tom, Edward and even Irwin felt they should do something about it. Business premises were generally insured. When Carrs Hardware Stores, Scollards Tailors and J.T. Mowats Wool Store burnt down early in the year, possibly, vaguely possibly, wet wool and spontaneous combustion may have started the fire. Three months later houses and shops were set alight. Worse still, Jamie, making sure as his father had before him, that the occupants were safely out of their dwellings, found one of the owners gagged and bound to a chair in a house already aflame in one corner. Then in September the Borough School was burnt down; no pupils there, thank goodness. A month later a big fire occurred in Earll and McKenzie's livery stables.

Jamie was growing tired of call-outs. 'They can't all be accidents, not four in less than a year,' he said. 'In fact, an accident, like that exploding tin of turpentine, is the first thing we hear about.'

In other ways he found Blenheim becoming even more prim. 'Stopping the s.s. *Kanieri* taking on coal during Sunday afternoon!' he exclaimed to Tom. 'It's mealy-mouthed. They even called out the police to stop it.' Whether

247

the coal came from Shakespeare Bay bound for Picton for cargo, or for bunkering for the ship, was never made clear to those who raised the question, as Jamie and Tom did.

There was still time for silly wrangles, much enjoyed by those not directly involved. Three men took a case to Court regarding the ownership of a swarm of bees. Edward relished Jamie's mathematical explanation: 'The swarm alighted on man A, who claimed that therefore it belonged to him. Man B claimed that since the bees swarmed from his hive they still belonged to him. And Man C' Jamie concluded in a domini's voice, 'had seen the swarm and followed it, so he claimed it as 'finders, keepers' '.

'How did the case end?' asked Tom when he had finished laughing.

Jamie joined in the laughter. 'There was no report of the outcome,' he replied. 'Well, that's what the paper said.'

Ken had been frustrated in his efforts for the community. The final straw for him was when the government building was turned over to the army, so that local body meetings could be made to close at 10 p.m., at the point of a bayonet if necessary. The members of the Blenheim Rifles were given authority to expel any board or council, or any member that refused to leave.

'A physical closure' Ken snarled. 'We're just puppets.'

'You'd do better in Wellington, Ken,' his wife said. 'They're old diehards here, you'll never change them.'

Ken looked at her with a smile. 'You'd like that city, too, wouldn't you, my dear?'

'Next thing your wife will say women manage things better than men,' Edward remarked.

'We would,' said Jean firmly.

'Votes for women-um-yes, perhaps,' Ken agreed. 'I've heard there's a movement in favour, Hall's behind it.'

The conversation dropped; but it left its mark. The three other couples began to think it would not be long before they lost Ken and Sarah to the 'windy city'.

Winter brought more diphtheria, with schools closed for three weeks. Mary, still with vivid recollections once again of little Jeanie's death, would not stir from the house. Every drop of water was boiled; William's bathwater was boiled. Mary had forgotten, if she had ever been aware of it, that well-water was the suspect, especially in low-lying areas of poor sanitation, not tank water. Down the road Sarah, with a child at school, was ignored. Jamie's twins, much younger, were welcomed with their parents. Both Mary and

Irwin felt that the danger lurked in schools; they may have been right, certainly the epidemic spread more quickly among school children. They sighed with relief when the school bells rang again. For the time being the community was in the clear.

By the following year the doctors had produced a report that horrified and damned the Council, condemning poor sewerage, stagnant water and cess pools. These statements had been obvious to eye and nose during an earlier flood, when the *Express* failed to go to press on account of excess moisture. The report could more briefly have read: 'Flooded out, again.' And Councils had been horrified before, and often, during at least two decades.

Jean was always the one to find some bright side to life. She coaxed Mary and Hannah to watch a team of fifteen grocers play football against fifteen drapers. The drapers were very elegant in dress, but the grocers, used to sides of bacon and hundredweights of sugar and flour, were much more successful physically. On the other hand, Jean had no idea which team had won.

Henry and Tom Newman's mail coach from Nelson was no longer a novelty. But welcoming Tom's first coachload of tourists from Nelson was an outing to remember; six o'clock on a summer's evening brought men as well as women to see the four splendid matched greys, and to watch the weary travellers descend after their eleven hour journey. The more nervous passengers had almost forgotten their fears above the deep gorges, where the two leaders could be out of sight so sharp were the corners, in the last eleven spanking miles across the Wairau Plain.

Jean lingered by the coach; her two youngest, both married, were working in Nelson. She was eager to see them. No longer was there a rough sea voyage ahead, with two, perhaps three changes of vessel, because rarely was there a direct Blenheim to Nelson sailing. Maybe they could save enough money for the coach fare. But Maisie was here in Blenheim; those two little grandchildren held a special place in her heart. Sometimes she almost envied Mary, with lively William to bring sunlight to days that grew steadily longer as duties grew less. How Mary managed she never ceased to wonder, with that silent, sometimes sullen, husband of hers. At least, when he had wandered off to Mahikapawa to fossick for gold he had told them all where he was heading.

Tom and Ken could put up with his silences; Edward Pascoe, not very talkative himself, was also reserved. Was it a Cornish trait? Jean wondered. But no; Mary, when she felt well, could be equally as much of a chatterbox as Jean herself, and Cornish born Sarah also.

Ken was spending more time in the Capital City. He was tired of mental brick walls, he told Edward. Everything one tried to do for the community was thwarted by man or nature: fires, epidemics, floods. 'Look what happened when they tried to get a decent water-supply,' he continued. 'Drill 315 feet for an artesian supply, the pipe breaks, and there's an end of it. There's over 3000 of us living here, mainly dependent on shallow wells with God knows what suspect water.'

Sarah hinted openly that they might leave the township soon; the group that had been friends for nearly thirty years was breaking up.

'We never see Ray or Polly now,' Irwin said out of the blue one day.

'Or our Margaret,' said Mary sadly.

'Would you like to see them?' What a stupid question. Irwin was as insensitive as ever.

'All that way and back, we couldn't. Not to Margaret's, anyway,' Mary said.

'Well, I'm like Ken, I want to get out of this place, for a while. Ken tells me they want a couple at the Acheron Accommodation House.'

'What about William?'

'He'd be all right. I know you set store on schooling, but he wouldn't miss much.'

'And he'd always be missing it here, anyway,' responded Mary. 'If it isn't floods, it's epidemics, or the school's burned down.' That was an unfair comment; the school itself had been destroyed by fire only once, so far.

'Well, Mary, would you cook for the drovers at Acheron?' It was probably the first time he had asked a question about their future rather than make a statement.

'Do we have to ride up the Waihopai again?'

'No, there's a bullock track in the Upper Awatere, and the coach takes us through to Langridge. It only takes two days with the mail.'

'And how long would you want to stay?'

'Well, I hadn't thought. A few months. Perhaps more.'

'What about our home while we're away, Irwin?'

'Jamie and Maisie might like to live here, for the winter at least. They're a bit too near the Taylor for my liking, with the twins so small,' Irwin replied.

20

As swiftly as that Mary and Irwin decided. She could perhaps see Margaret, too, down the Acheron and over the Clarence to Hanmer. After all the troubles with the bullock track through the cuttings, the road was now open in summer.

They set off by coach, luxurious travelling compared with the past; over the Dashwood, preferred to the Taylor and up the Awatere, with its now well-established stations: Burtergill, Altimarloch, Upton Downs, Jordan, Upcot, mail for each of them. Mary found it difficult to remember all the names, while she contrasted the speed of the horses with the slow plodding bullocks she had known.

Two days they spent with Ray and Polly and their family far up the valley, their first real holiday, Mary told her friend. Young William scuttled over the home paddocks with Polly's children; he had not known such freedom. The country looked much more tamed and prosperous, but Ray reminded them the winters were just as savage as ever.

Fowler at Molesworth had been using phosphorised pollard against the rabbits, succeeding to some extent in retaining pasture for sheep. As Ken had said, it was not sheep country, even for merinos. Fine stands of trees for firewood and shelter had developed since the first plantings, after Fuhrmann and Willis had bought the Molesworth Run from Atkinson. A wagon-load of green willows from Altimarloch added colour now to the bare hillsides. The Trelissicks found it hard to recognise what had been their home, with the Taylor homestead the focal point on the Crown Grant of 1027 acres.

Then by bullock wagon down the Acheron, through those cuttings which had caused Tarndale so much conflict.

The Accommodation House, twenty-five years after Irwin had first clambered, wet and tired, into a box bed, was much better equipped. After the confined cob cottage, the eight rooms amazed Mary at first; but she felt they could quite comfortably settle there for some years. Once the drovers began coming through, she was very busy cooking huge meals; by evening often all the beds were in use, latecomers spreading sacks on the floor. The kitchen steamed with the stockpot, iron saucepans jammed the range top, the oven was always in use. Irwin was chopping wood at all hours; Mary could not stop to fill the woodbox, that task belonged to William. She was busy, happy, no time to be concerned about her quiet husband; no time to consider a reason for his brown bear moods. They overtook him less frequently here with the passing travellers bringing new interests.

William's schooling problem was solved as soon as Mary had three days free to make that longed for visit to Hanmer, where Margaret, whose husband farmed nearby, met her. Little brother was most welcome; the school was near enough for him to ride there, on a quiet pony they had bought for their younger children in the future. It would be a great help for Midget to be ridden regularly, added Margaret, brushing aside her mother's gratitude. Mary did not want to burden her daughter, with her own babies to care for and a hard-working husband; perhaps after the winter, she finally agreed.

Winter was less harsh at the lower level of the Acheron. Still the Clarence was often too high for the wayfarers to cross, or snow made the passes too treacherous. But the thick rammed earth walls and the abundance of firewood kept the building warm. Both Irwin and Mary enjoyed the occasional company. It was a different world, not quite solitary but quiet enough to suit them both, older with hardship than their actual age. They began to feel that they could settle here for the rest of their lives.

The Clarence Valley had a soothing tranquil quality in late spring, with the blue peaks far above still snow-capped. The full length of the Inland Kaikouras hid them from Tapuaenuku and its shadows.

21

A tiny quiver of thunder far away, no lightning. Maisie on this warm February morning in Blenheim listened: it was rumbling around the Wairau hills. She opened the door; the sky was cloudless. At least there could not be another flood.

The rumble persisted, the air quivered more noticeably. Two cups on the shelf chattered. She looked more closely, the shelf was tipping. No, she must be feeling faint. A little jolt shook the house; her mother had talked to her about earthquakes. But they were always such tiny things, not nearly as worrying as floods. There had been one that brought a few chimneys down; poorly built they were, her father had mentioned, she thought vaguely.

One of the twins had wakened. Nearly time for their meal, they took long enough over it.

Jamie had left for work an hour earlier. What had he said about that Landseer print on the wall, just above where they had put the cots in this house that belonged to his people? As Maisie's world tilted again, she stumbled uphill on the wooden floor to scoop up a twin

258

under each arm. Behind her, as she turned away, the oak-framed print crashed onto the little pillow.

Where should she go under this suddenly darkened sky in the horrid tumbling and clattering? Bricks cascaded outside as the chimney collapsed, like the twins' blocks towering out of balance. The attic creaked above them. The kerosene lamp, with its painted glass of which her mother-in-law was so proud, swung off its ceiling hook, crashing on the floor; in a sub-conscious moment Maisie was glad Jamie had forgotten to fill it the night before. In the kitchen, in all this slow swinging and shaking and the hiccough-ing jolt at the end of each tremor, the shelves were swept clean in a crash that destroyed all the summer's hot work of preserving. Maisie, burdened with the twins, stepped out of the way of the tall dresser that teetered and fell across the doorway.

To the backdoor, then — but the chimney? Could it fall that way? And was the stove out? Could she smell burning? A window cracked like the snap of kindling well alight. Jane's trundle bed made up its mind to career across the floor, coming to a sudden stop as the tremor ceased.

Maisie found herself in the orchard, the twins bawling for that meal she had planned to give them how long ago? She had lost count of time. Four hundred gallons of concertina'd water tank had gouged a river in the vegetable garden. She could see great cracks in the street, and across the road the wall of a house had fallen outwards.

Over the town hung a pall of smoke; she could hear the fire bell, still crazily pealing from the quake, an alarm without the volunteers ringing it. Jamie — where was he?

Grimy, soot-blackened from chimneys where ranges were still alight for late breakfasts or baking, he appeared two hours later; fire-fighting had to come before the family, unless the members were thought to be in danger. He was so thankful to find them there in the orchard.

As soon as he judged it safe, they looked at the shambles. Maisie burst into tears over the ruins of those long hours of bottling fruit and making jam, everything flung from the pantry shelves in a welter of broken jars and crocks, ruining the dry goods — flour, sugar, oatmeal — on the way down.

'Your mother's home,' sobbed Maisie, 'and I did try to look after it. Look. I'll never be able to set it to rights. What will she think of me?'

'My dear,' her husband said, 'mother will understand. No-one could help this. They'll be thankful you and the twins are safe. Life is what matters most with everyone.'

'And, Jamie, what about our own home?'

'I don't know yet. I came straight to you as soon as we were sure that all the fires were dowsed, and no-one trapped anywhere under falling beams. We've had a quite a time of it.'

'But what do you think will have happened? Will it be as bad as this?'

'I'm afraid so. Very few homes haven't been damaged.'

Indeed, the young folk's home was in worse condition; it had not been so soundly built in the first place. There, too, all Maisie's hard work had been wasted. She had been storing up preserves so that both households would be well provided with fruit should her husband's parents return to Blenheim before the next bottling season.

Looking at the wreckage of their home, Maisie said, 'I can't keep a nice home in Blenheim, Jamie, really I can't. If it's not flood, it's earthquakes or the threat of fires. We no sooner get things right than we have more trouble.'

'I know, my dear,' Jamie soothed her. 'And I know the twins take a lot of your time, too. I've been quietly thinking about a move to Christchurch. How would you like that idea?' Jamie was unlike his father; the young couple made their decisions together, unusual in the late Victorian era, where throughout most of his parents' lives, Irwin had decided on future plans.

Her tears and the disaster forgotten, she flew into his arms. 'That would be wonderful. When can we go?'

'Not for a while, Maisie. I've not told you earlier because I was waiting to be sure of a job.'

'And you are now?' Her eyes shone with excitement.

'It's almost certain. Ed has been making enquiries for me. Be patient a little longer, dear, don't tell your mother yet.'

'It's going to be hard on her, and father.'

'And my people, too,' Jamie pointed out.

'At least they've already left Blenheim.'

'Yes. But we'll have to tell them about this. There's a crying need for carpenters in town. Some people are facing much more damage than we are, specially where those ranges were still alight when chimneys fell. And there's our home as well as theirs. I can't repair both in a hurry, on my own.'

'But it's summer, Jamie,' Maisie objected. 'Can't you do ours first, then your people's later on?'

'Father is a lot handier than I am. And if that job in Christchurch comes up in a week

262

or two, as it might, we can't leave either house open to the weather — windows and chimneys, and any walls that need extra support, before we get any heavy rain, or floods.'

'You're — you're not thinking there might be another flood before we leave?'

'You'll hear about it in town, so I had better tell you, Maisie dear. They think there might have been a change in the river-beds, might be good news, might be bad. We just have to wait and see. But none of us in those lower areas dare take a chance on it.'

22

It seemed to Mary and Irwin that they were no sooner in the flow of summer travellers than Ray rode down from the Awatere. In week-old Canterbury newspapers the Trelissicks had learned that there had been quite a heavy shock along the Wairau fault line. Not having suffered more than minor shocks themselves, they took little notice of the news Mary read to her husband. Any reference to damage to buildings Irwin dismissed with a comment to the effect that shoddy workmanship was probably the cause.

Ray's news put an end to their tranquillity. Jamie had sent a message through as soon as the mail could reach Langridge; the Awatere had suffered, also. His parents' house was damaged, his own little flood-prone cottage worse, nothing except basic repair would make it fit to live in until winter. He would do his best, but there was so much to be done, with a shortage of labour in the building trade. Jamie did not need to tell Ray that he would do his best; Ray knew.

The next part of the message would have

sent Mary back post-haste in any case, to see as much of the twins before Jamie took up this new job he mentioned in Christchurch. He had decided it was only fair to warn his mother about the move, with the job almost definite once postal services began flowing again. Both homes could be made habitable; would his parents want to return from Acheron? Neighbours and friends were all in the same position. Needed were extra pairs of hands, with windows to be glazed, chimneys rebuilt, most important of all tank stands shored up and collapsed tanks replaced, for those with or without access to doubtful wells.

Maisie decided to move back to their more flood-prone home, although there would have been cramped room to stay with Jamie's parents. Irwin and Mary gave short notice at the Acheron Accommodation House.

By late autumn the Taylor was 200 yards wide. Jamie and Maisie, with the twins and what they could carry, waded through before their garden was ankle-deep, to stay with the senior Trelissicks. Whether the earthquake had altered the bed of the river no-one could say; but surprisingly the cob cottage was not flooded even to floor-level, although the platform of the band rotunda was under water.

On top of that, another epidemic — measles this time — closed the schools. Jean was tireless; one little grandson was very ill, complications from the disease turning to pneumonia, until they all wondered if the beloved child would pull through. The other twin, thanks be, had a very mild infection.

William also was very ill; Mary wished most fervently that she had let him stay with Margaret in North Canterbury. Jean tried to help Mary as well as daughter Maisie. All of them were praying that there would not be another sad little grave in the cemetery, or a partially-sighted child.

Convalescence for both children was only just a thing of the past when the shops were under water again. A month or so later, fire broke out, but this time at least the arsonist was not at work. Ken explained that a tin of turpentine had exploded in the paint store. Jamie was suspicious: a second tin exploding in the store? Why?

His appointment in Christchurch had been confirmed. Maisie had begun to wonder if it would ever happen; or, indeed, if all the family would be alive to shift south. Neither of the Trelissick's or indeed Jean and Tom, had many regrets. Some areas were much healthier and safer than

Blenheim, they were deciding.

'Perhaps in another twenty years,' said Ed, 'everything will be sorted out. After all, the problems are mainly caused by rivers and sewage. It could be a lovely place to live. Come back in 1915, Jamie.'

When Jamie had first discussed his move with his father, Irwin said, 'I don't blame you. I'd leave here, if your mother would board ship. But she vowed when we landed that here she would stay, and she's stuck to it.'

The son was taken aback; it was unusual for his father to speak so openly. After all, mother had twice gone into the back country with him. Did his mother know what his father was thinking? And did he really understand his wife at all? After all — Jamie's thoughts went on piling up in a series of after alls — what someone said thirty years earlier, after a dreadful voyage, was not necessarily a determination so much later, and after so many demanding hardships. His mother hated the floods and fires and epidemics, and the earthquakes. Had she talked about that to his father? Jamie wondered if anyone could have a real discussion with his father before he shuffled quietly into that brown bear mood. Surely Maisie would always be able to express her thoughts and feelings to her husband?

Mary watched the family board one of Captain Eckford's ships. Jamie was going to a well-paid permanent job. And here in Blenheim the council had allocated only twenty-five sovereigns to pay the unemployed to break metal on the roads. And the twins would be beyond the reach of all these natural disasters, she considered, plodding back home with William skipping on ahead.

More moody than ever, Irwin still would not speak out. In the rush of their departure, Jamie had not made the opportunity to hint to his mother that father would like to leave the district permanently.

The summer flood would have been enough for Sarah and Ken, without their son's discovery of the body of a murdered man in the Opawa River. Some down-and-outer with a tiny speck of gold in his pocket; he was never identified. Was Blenheim harbouring a murderer as well as an arsonist? It was all very well for the police to say that the double murder at Tophouse a few months earlier had been committed by the suicide that followed it. But had it been? Was the crime hushed up? They'd need to lock their doors soon; this wasn't the friendly, family town they had known.

A second heavy earthquake sent Ken and Sarah to their packing; they were on the train to Picton with their family before the town for which he had tried to do so much had time to give them the customary farewell.

Still Mary and Irwin kept their thoughts to themselves. Jamie and Maisie gone, George in Christchurch and Brenda nursing there, where Jane had joined her, Margaret in North Canterbury. Mary often thought in desperation that there was nothing of value left in Blenheim.

Jean broke down the wall of silence between the couple when again all the streets were impassable in July. The water lapped the doorstep at Trelissick's; the white fence, the pickets hand-turned by Irwin, would need the silt scrubbed off them yet again. Tom was sitting there, too; nothing to do but visit until the flood waters receded, as in the old days, though it was no longer in a crowd on the second floor of the hotel.

'What keeps you two here with William?' Jean asked abruptly. 'Us?'

Irwin, surprised, glanced at Mary.

'Yes,' said Tom, 'do you really want to hang on here, Irwin? I'm damned if I do — sorry, Mary — but I'm fed up, and so is Jean.'

'I must tell you, Mary, we've been through such a lot together. Tom and I have talked about it, and we're leaving soon. We'll all be away, except Hannah and Ed Pascoe.'

'I thought you might move. Where will you go?'

'Tom and I think we'll go to Nelson. The boys are there, and their wives are nice girls,' Jean replied.

Nelson — by coach. Mary wouldn't need to board a ship. Irwin turned the idea over in his mind; he'd ask her about it some day.

But some day did not come. Another flood, before the earlier one had dried out properly, saw Mary in one of her rare tempestuous moods. The streets were a quagmire, her spring garden ruined. 'I'm sick of playing at beavers,' she told Jean. 'Better to put up with snow for weeks on end at Molesworth.'

Tom and Jean had packed up, ready to leave the desolate community behind them. The gas explosion in the Bank of New Zealand was their farewell.

Irwin had gone to Newmans with Tom, to help with the luggage, and Mary, too. William was dragging along with them, he liked Auntie Jean and Uncle Tom; no school during and just after floods, for fear of further epidemics.

The thought of plodding back in the slush and mud to another fire, another flood, more epidemics, perhaps more earthquakes was too much for Mary. Patience snapped, along with the Victorian promise to obey her husband and her determination to remain at his side. The Nelson coach pulled out. She marched William with her to the offices on the river wharf.

Irwin watched her. What was she doing?

They walked home silently. Mary sent William up to the attic bedroom, all his own now, the others would never come back. Jane might return some day. Or would she? The copper still stood in the middle of a flooded backyard.

Would her husband ask her what she had been doing at the shipping company's offices? No. He had retreated to his brown bear mood. Was he ever in a different frame of mind these days, she wondered, even for a moment or two?

Mary grabbed at the remnants of her self-control. 'You won't ask, and you won't discuss things with me. Now I'm telling you: William and I are going to Christchurch, for keeps. I've saved enough money.

'But,' he argued, 'you said you'd never go on a boat again.'

'Oh, Irwin — ' half-sobbing, half-angry, she tried to make this obstinate man of hers understand, 'fires and floods and epidemics. And you expect me to stay here because of what I said thirty years ago. I want hills, hills, above the floods, the hills of Home . . . '

'We could never go back there,' Irwin replied, more gently than he had ever spoken.

'I know. And if we could, I wouldn't leave our family for a land across the sea. But Brenda says there are hills round Christchurch, and a little port, like pictures she's seen of our Cornish coast.'

'I'll tell you now,' he admitted slowly, 'I've wanted to leave here for years, but we could never afford it. Why d'you think I went away looking for gold? And took us back to the Acheron and the Clarence?'

'But you said that would be only for a short time,' Mary argued.

'Um — I was thinking we might go over the Pass to Hanmer; but I knew you wanted to be near Jamie's twins, I thought you wouldn't come with me.'

'I'll go without you,' she said firmly, 'if you won't come, too.'

Captain Eckford's *Neptune* took them down river on the turn of the tide. Not much to show for thirty-five years on the Wairau Plains, those open sweeps of earlier wasteland, swamps of flax and toi toi. Somewhere upriver was the forgotten ten acres that had brought them 12,000 miles from the land of their birth.

The steamer rolled on the swell, flying a

big mainsail to steady her on her voyage south across the Canterbury Bight, the snowcaps of Tapuaenuku in sight until they changed course to enter Lyttelton Harbour.

THE END

We do hope that you have enjoyed reading this large print book.

Did you know that all of our titles are available for purchase?

We publish a wide range of high quality large print books including:
Romances, Mysteries, Classics
General Fiction
Non Fiction and Westerns

Special interest titles available in large print are:
The Little Oxford Dictionary
Music Book
Song Book
Hymn Book
Service Book

Also available from us courtesy of Oxford University Press:
Young Readers' Dictionary
(large print edition)
Young Readers' Thesaurus
(large print edition)

For further information or a free brochure, please contact us at:
Ulverscroft Large Print Books Ltd.,
The Green, Bradgate Road, Anstey,
Leicester, LE7 7FU, England.
Tel: (00 44) 0116 236 4325
Fax: (00 44) 0116 234 0205